Praise for *The E...*

"For all LGBTQ+ teens and young adults, this book will help inspire and empower you to become your best selves. This book shares how the LGBTQ+ community has made invaluable contributions. It throws open the doors of queer possibility, making it clear we can use our imagination to make distinctive marks on our world however we choose."

—Dustin Lance Black,
Academy Award-winning Screenwriter, *Milk*

"The need for positive role models in the LGBTQ+ Community has never been greater. In a divisive political climate, books like this one encourage and inspire LGBTQ+ youth to focus on their part in advancing society. Whether in science, technology, education, sports, government or the arts, the LGBTQ+ community has made an indelible mark on the world. Undaunted by prejudice, marginalization, discrimination and violence, the community has persisted and dedicated its efforts to the greater good. In the words of MLK Jr., 'the arc of the moral universe is long, but it bends toward justice.'"

—Libby Schaaf,
Mayor of Oakland, 2015–2023

"When President Barack Obama came to our school system to highlight our early childhood programs, I had the privilege of representing Clairemont Elementary School. As a lifetime teacher, I so appreciate a book that shines a light on a previously marginalized community. We are an inclusive school system and this book can give us tools to expand the dialogue about history and change."

—Stephanie Trauner,
Retired teacher, Clairemont Elementary,
A Blue Ribbon school, in Decatur, Georgia

"Throughout history, the LGBTQ+ community has been erased, marginalized or vilified. Since the passing of the F.A.I.R. Education Act in California, that wrong is being corrected at long last. The inclusion of the contributions of the LGBTQ+

community to society is required to be taught in history and social studies classes in California public schools. This book shines a spotlight on the amazing contributions of our community. School kids will learn that we are more than the stereotypes the media has projected and how our dedicated efforts in a variety of fields have enhanced the common good."

—Dr. Ardel Thomas,
Chair, LGBTQ+ Studies, CCSF

"Give this book to the young people in your life! It will offer inspiration regardless of their sexual orientation or gender identity. For LGBTQIA young people in particular—for whom coming out can be a tremendously isolating experience filled with uncertainty—this book provides a glimpse into the lives of well-known LGBTQIA people who live full, productive and happy lives, providing hope and strength for their journey as they grow into their blessed, God-created selves."

—Bishop Karen Oliveto, PhD,
First Openly Lesbian United Methodist Church Bishop,
Author, *Together at the Table: Diversity Without Division in the United Methodist Church*

"At IBM, we value diversity and have lived our values, leading the technology industry with our forward-thinking practices and policies. Not only great for the LGBTQ+ Community, but great for our business. This book demonstrates that being LGBTQ+ does not have to inhibit, but can, in fact, enhance your career. When you can be your authentic self, you are your best self."

—Claudia Brind-Woody, Esq.,
Co-Chair Executive Diversity Leadership Council
IBM VP of Global Intellectual Property Licensing

"Growing up in my Maori indigenous culture of New Zealand and with a father who was a leader of our local marae, sacred communal gathering place for over thirty years, I lived the value of community. We believe that we are never alone, our ancestors are always with us and so we share a collective, interconnected identity that helps us to stand strong in solidarity with our ancestors. This book may help you to remember

that we are all connected to a global Rainbow family. Find our people—within family, friends, teachers, coaches, counselors, pastors who will support you and help you on your sexual orientation and gender identity journey. We are the potential of our ancestors, free and equal and we are never alone."

—Louisa Wall,
Ambassador for Gender Equality (2022–2024) and
former Member of New Zealand Parliment (2011–2022)

"Right now, more than ever, we need these stories of sheroes and heroes and gender-expansive warriors to inspire us on our paths toward justice. Kathleen and Eric have eloquently lifted up these stories for all of our benefit, showing us queer and trans people as powerful agents of change, love and liberation."

—Sean Dorsey,
Trans Choreographer and Activist
Founder and Artistic Director, Fresh Meat Productions

"This book should be required reading in schools and homes. All people—however they are born—should be free to reach their full potential. It is only an uninformed society which creates hurdles in this direction. Here we have the evidence that sexual orientation need not get in the way of success. Let us celebrate and speak about the high achievements of these great people, in the hope that they will be an inspiration to LGBTIQ youth. I thank the authors for creating this platform to commemorate these accomplishments."

—Dr. Helena Dalli,
Minister for European Affairs and Equality,
Holder of European Diversity Award

THE
BOOK OF
AWESOME
QUEER
HEROES

Also by These Authors

Eric Rosswood

Queer Cheer: Activities, Advice, and Affirmations for LGBTQ+ Teens

The Ultimate Guide for Gay Dads: Everything You Need to Know About LGBTQ Parenting But Are (Mostly) Afraid to Ask

Journey to Parenthood: The Ultimate Guide for Same-Sex Couples

My Uncle's Wedding

STRONG

Kathleen Archambeau

Pride & Joy: LGBTQ Artists, Icons and Everyday Heroes

"Seized," an essay in The Other Woman, edited by Victoria Zackheim

Climbing the Corporate Ladder in High Heels

THE BOOK OF AWESOME QUEER HEROES

How the LGBTQ+ Community Changed the World for the Better

Eric Rosswood
and
Kathleen Archambeau

MIAMI

Cover Design: Jodie Anders
Layout & Design: Roberto Núñez

For permission requests, please contact the publisher at:
Mango Publishing Group
5966 South Dixie Highway, Suite 300
Miami, FL 33143
info@mango.bz

For special orders, quantity sales, course adoptions and corporate sales, please
email the publisher at sales@mango.bz. For trade and wholesale sales, please
contact Ingram Publisher Services at customer.service@ingramcontent.com or
+1.800.509.4887.

The Book of Awesome Queer Heroes: How the LGBTQ+ Community
Changed the World for the Better

Library of Congress Cataloging-in-Publication: 2024943930
ISBN: (p) 978-1-68481-689-7 (e) 978-1-68481-690-3
BISAC category code YAN006150, YOUNG ADULT NONFICTION /
Biography & Autobiography / LGBTQ+

Dedicated to all LGBTQ+ youth with big dreams. May this book help you reach your potential and find your place in the world. You are valid, you are loved, and you are part of something bigger. Together #WeMakeItBetter.

Table of Contents

FOREWORD

by
Kate Kendell, Esq.

When I was growing up Mormon in Utah, I never imagined I would become a lawyer leading one of the largest LGBTQ+ legal organizations in the country, the National Center for Lesbian Rights (NCLR). Growing up, I never saw my parents read serious books or, in my dad's case, even the newspapers. No one in my community, schools, or neighborhood ever acknowledged the existence of queer people. My parents never had a passport. A trip to Hawaii my dad won through his work as an insurance agent when I was thirteen was the first time I'd been on a plane.

At the University of Utah Law School, I and two other closeted friends kept our sexual orientation to ourselves. When I landed a position at one of the most prestigious law firms in Salt Lake City, I remained in the closet for fear of losing my job. Three years later, as the first staff attorney for the American Civil Liberties Union of Utah, I found my voice and, once found, that voice only grew. In 1994, I began my career in activism as legal director of the National Center for Lesbian Rights in San Francisco. In 1996, I became the Executive Director of NCLR and held that position for twenty-two years.

While at NCLR, we battled and won the right to marry in California in 2013 and, again, nationally in 2015. We won parental and hospital visitation rights, child custody rights, senior housing rights, protections for LGBTQ+ youth, transgender health care, many cases for LGBTQ+ immigrants, and much more in those twenty-two years. But as much progress as we made, it is clear to me today that our victories are fragile and vulnerable.

In 2024, LGBTQ+ lives and dignity are being relentlessly attacked. LGBTQ+ youth of color are particularly vulnerable. PEN America identified more than four thousand instances of book banning during the first half of the 2023–2024 school year, with almost half of those bans due to LGBTQ+ themes or titles. Nearly half of US states allow the harmful pseudoscientific practice of conversion therapy. Transgender children and their parents are denied healthcare access in many states, resulting in arrests, school bullying, and youth suicide. Globally, queer people continue to be violently attacked, imprisoned, and murdered.

Never before has it been more crucial to support queer youth. This book not only informs but celebrates the contributions of queer heroes in all major fields of endeavor. From religion to the military, from government to the arts, from science to health and technology, from entertainment to film, unsung queer heroes take center stage. I'm proud to encourage teachers, students, parents, government leaders, corporate executives, and kids to read about the amazing contributions of queer icons, not only to the LGBTQ+ community but to the community at large. You will be astounded and inspired. The hope I still carry is due to these individuals and their remarkable stories.

Kate Kendell, Esq., was the executive director of the National Center for Lesbian Rights from 1996 to 2018. She currently serves as the first chief of staff for The California Endowment, the largest health justice foundation in California.

INTRODUCTION

How LGBTQ+ People Make the World a Better Place

You probably learned about Martin Luther King Jr. in school. History books teach us that he was one of the most visible leaders of the Civil Rights Movement, but did you know that Bayard Rustin, one of King's most trusted mentors and advisors, was an openly gay man? Rustin was instrumental in organizing the march on Washington where King gave his famous "I Have a Dream" speech. Rustin also played an important role in the Civil Rights Movement, but much of what he did was behind the scenes.

We've all learned about World War II in school as well, but did you know Alan Turing, another openly gay man, deciphered German codes that were significant in helping us win the war? LGBTQ+ people like Bayard Rustin and Alan Turing have played important roles in history. People in our community have made, and continue to make, significant contributions to the world. For example, Sally Ride was the first American woman in space, and was also the first known LGBTQ+ astronaut. Apple, the largest tech company in the world, is run by Tim Cook, an openly gay man. Under his leadership, Apple became the first publicly traded US company to hit a market value of one trillion dollars. When it comes to sports, Megan Rapinoe is an Olympic gold medalist who fought for equal pay for women in US soccer and won. The Wachowskis are transgender siblings who directed *The Matrix*, which became one of the biggest blockbuster sci-fi movie franchises ever created, and Jóhanna Sigurðardóttir was the world's first openly gay head of government and Iceland's first female prime minister. That's right, we even run countries.

Did they teach you about any of these accomplishments in your school textbooks? Probably not. For some reason, there are people who have gone to great lengths to minimize or hide the accomplishments of LGBTQ+ people. Many of them have even taken it a step further.

Have you ever heard the phrase "No Promo Homo" before? It's a phrase used to describe laws that prohibit the "promotion of homosexuality" in schools. Some of these laws ban teachers from discussing LGBTQ+ people in a positive light, and others even require teachers to portray LGBTQ+ people in a negative way.

The UK had its own version of this type of law in Section 28 (or Clause 28) of the Local Government Act of 1988. The amendment stated that a local authority "shall not intentionally promote homosexuality or publish material with the intention of promoting homosexuality" and a local authority "shall not promote the teaching of the acceptability of homosexuality as a pretended family relationship in any maintained school." Section 28 was repealed in Scotland in 2000 and the rest of the UK in 2003, but these types of laws still exist in various countries around the world.

Russia has implemented a variety of provisions restricting expression, assembly, and funding, and support groups for LGBTQ+ youth are illegal in the country because they are thought to promote "nontraditional sexual relations among minors." In the United States, more than thirty anti-LGBTQ+ laws restricting LGBTQ+ topics in schools were enacted in 2023 alone. Alabama State Code § 16-40A-2(c)(8) even goes as far as to state that classes should emphasize "in a factual manner and from a public health perspective that homosexuality is not a lifestyle acceptable to the general public, and that homosexual conduct is a criminal offense under the laws of the state." US politicians and activists have also turned their focus to book bans. According to Pen America, there were over four thousand instances of book banning during the first half of the 2023–24 school year, with a huge number of them focusing on books with queer themes or queer content.

In addition to all of this, almost half of the United States still allow conversion therapy, the harmful pseudoscience quackery that falsely claims to be able to change the sexual orientation, gender identity, or gender expression of LGBTQ+ people. The Williams Institute published a study in 2018 that revealed an "estimated twenty thousand LGBTQ+ youth in the US, ages thirteen to seventeen, will receive conversion therapy from a licensed health care professional before the age of eighteen" and "approximately fifty-seven thousand youth will undergo the treatment from a religious or spiritual advisor."

Why is it that some governments go out of their way to prevent people from talking about LGBTQ+ people, and in other cases, even try to convert us? People in the LGBTQ+ community have made positive contributions throughout history and we continue to improve society today. We set trends in fashion, film, music, art, and technology. We're Academy Award winners, Grammy Award winners, Pulitzer Prize winners, and Olympic gold medalists. We're doctors, lawyers, judges, politicians, and religious leaders. We run businesses, and we even run countries.

It is important to feature LGBTQ+ role models and highlight their contributions to society. That's why we created this book, to shine a light on some of these remarkable queer trailblazers

THE BOOK OF AWESOME QUEER HEROES

and their significant contributions to society through bite-sized, easily comprehensible, mini profiles. Hopefully, these stories will inspire people around the world and help them realize that being LGBTQ+ is something to celebrate. Our community has made significant contributions to society, and that's something to be proud of, not to hide in the closet. We're here, we're queer, and we make the world a better place. #WeMakeItBetter.

Part 1

ACTIVISM

Marsha P. Johnson and Sylvia Rivera

LGBTQ+ Equality Activists

"You never completely have your rights, one person, until you all have your rights."

–Marsha P. Johnson

"Hell hath no fury like a drag queen scorned."

–Sylvia Rivera

M arsha P. Johnson was born on August 24, 1945, in Elizabeth, New Jersey. She was assigned male at birth and started wearing dresses around age five, but stopped after being bullied by other kids. At seventeen years old, she moved to New York City with one bag of clothes and only fifteen dollars. Without much money, Johnson had to live on the streets. She had a rough life, but she found joy living as a drag queen, and, over time, she became a prominent fixture in the city's queer community.

Johnson served as a drag mother, helping other homeless and struggling queer teens. Not long after arriving in the city, she met a young Sylvia Rivera, and the two of them became friends. Johnson took Rivera under her wing and taught her how to wear makeup, live on the streets, look out for trouble, and, most importantly, how to love herself. Even though Johnson and Rivera were both homeless, they had passion in their hearts and a fire inside that motivated them to fight for LGBTQ+ rights, resulting in them both becoming prominent figures in LGBTQ+ history.

On June 28, 1969, the police raided the Stonewall Inn, one of the few gay bars in NYC. They roughly hauled people out of the bar, sparking a riot among patrons who were tired of police harassment. Protests and clashes with the police lasted for six days and served as the catalyst for the LGBTQ+ rights movement. There are many conflicting stories about how the uprising started, but it's clear that Johnson and Rivera emerged as influential leaders in the fight for LGBTQ+ equality.

In the wake of the riots, Johnson and Rivera participated in numerous rallies and protests for LGBTQ+ rights. They also joined emerging gay rights organizations, but those groups started putting trans people on the sidelines and focused on getting gay rights bills passed without the inclusion of trans protections. Johnson and Rivera knew trans people needed support too, so they helped found Street Transvestite Action Revolutionaries[1] to fight transphobia and offer food and shelter to homeless LGBTQ+ youth. Johnson and Rivera used their income from sex work to fund the STAR house so queer kids could sleep safely and hopefully avoid getting into trouble on the streets. The organization was revolutionary because it was the first time anyone had made a collective effort to support the homeless transgender community, especially trans youth.

Both Johnson and Rivera contributed significantly to the LGBTQ+ equality movement, marching for justice and organizing the community. Unfortunately, they both died far too young. In 1992, Johnson's body was found in the Hudson River with a large bruise on the back of her head. Authorities ruled her death a suicide, but the community suspected foul play. Rivera died ten years later of complications from liver cancer.

Johnson and Rivera have both been honored for their contributions in unique ways. In 2020, the East River State Park in Brooklyn, NY, was renamed the Marsha P. Johnson State Park, becoming the first NY state park named after an openly LGBTQ+ person. Johnson was also the subject of two documentaries: *Pay It No Mind—The Life and Times of Marsha P. Johnson* (2012) and *The Death and Life of Marsha P. Johnson* (2017). In 2005, the intersection of Christopher and Hudson Streets, two blocks from the Stonewall Inn, was renamed Sylvia Rivera Way. And the National Portrait Gallery added a portrait of Rivera in 2015, making her the first transgender activist to be included in the gallery.

---

1 The term "transgender" was not really used at the time STAR was founded and didn't become common until decades later. Johnson referred to herself as a gay person, a transvestite, and a drag queen. Rivera referred to herself as transgender later in life; however, she disliked labels.

Kelley Robinson

President of the Human Rights Campaign

"Together, we have all the power we need. And together, we will get to a world where we are free and liberated without exception—without exception—without anyone left behind."

Kelley Robinson knows how to organize. When she was a student at the University of Missouri, she became an activist and participated in various anti-discrimination campaigns on campus. Robinson later joined the Obama for America campaign as a community organizer where she focused on getting young people at local colleges registered to vote. Following that, she became the executive director of the Planned Parenthood Action Fund, and during her tenure, she quadrupled the fund to $45 million and shepherded the growth of the membership base from 6.5 million to 18 million. In 2022, after more than ten years working with Planned Parenthood, Robinson joined the Human Rights Campaign (HRC), the largest political LGBTQ+ lobbying and advocacy organization in the US, as the first Black, queer woman to lead the organization.

The HRC does more than lobby. Through its Equality Indexes, the organization reaches out to other organizations to help them track and improve their policies and practices when it comes to how they treat their LGBTQ+ employees, customers, citizens, vendors, and governing boards.

As a believer in intersectionality, Robinson sees her role as building partnerships and alliances across movements and uses her position to highlight the intersectional work needed on issues like LGBTQ+ equality, voting rights, gun control, racial justice, immigration, environmental justice, and more.

In 2023, Robinson took the bold step of declaring a national emergency for queer US citizens. She alerted the community to the crises faced with the rise in anti-LGBTQ+ violence, especially violence against Black transgender women. She also drew attention to the rise in book bans (most by or about BIPOC and queer authors and topics), anti-drag laws, the criminalization of trans healthcare, bullying, and discrimination. Robinson made numerous televised appearances to encourage people to get active, stand up to injustice, and vote. The nation was riled up and the majority of the anti-LGBTQ+ laws presented that year were defeated.

She was in the room in December of 2022 when the Respect for Marriage Act was signed by President Biden, enshrining more than a thousand rights for the LGBTQ+ community into law. Robinson, age thirty-eight, is married to Becky George, a first-generation American of South Asian descent and a senior advisor at Everytown for Gun Safety. The two of them have a son together so the bill was personal to them.

Because of her ability to build coalitions across intersecting issues and advance the larger social justice movement, Kelley Robinson was named one of *Time's* 100 Most Influential People in 2024. Today, she continues to expose injustices and fight for equality for all people without exception.

Bayard Rustin

Civil Rights Activist

"People will never fight for your freedom if you have not given evidence that you are prepared to fight for it yourself."

C hances are you've heard of Martin Luther King Jr. and his famous "I Have a Dream" speech, but did you know Bayard Rustin, an openly gay man, was a mentor to King and instrumental in organizing the March on Washington, where that speech was given?

Rustin, who was no stranger to fighting for equal rights, traveled to India in the 1940s and studied the nonviolent resistance practices taught by Mahatma Gandhi. He combined those teachings with the pacifism of the Quaker religion and the socialism supported by African-American labor leader A. Philip Randolph to come up with his own approach to fighting for equal rights. In the 1950s, he met Dr. Martin Luther King Jr. and advised him on the tactics of nonviolent civil disobedience.

As a mentor to King, Rustin helped him organize the successful Montgomery bus boycott, which ultimately led to the Supreme Court ruling it unconstitutional for Alabama and Montgomery to legally require segregation on their public transit system. He remained a close advisor to King for the next few years.

In the 1960s, Rustin became the Deputy Director for the March on Washington for Jobs and Freedom. He was a key strategist for the march, and, with his team, created and distributed a manual, which included demands and a roadmap that helped transform American civil rights, labor rights, and education and housing policies. This policy agenda played a crucial role in helping to secure passage of the Civil Rights Act of 1963 and the Voting Rights Act of 1964.

Rustin was involved in numerous boycotts and protests throughout his life, always fighting to protect and advance the rights of minority groups. He died in 1987 and was survived by Walter Naegle, his partner of ten years.

In 2013, Rustin was selected as an honoree in the United States Department of Labor Hall of Honor. That same year, President Obama posthumously awarded him the Presidential Medal of Freedom, the highest civilian award in the United States. Even though Rustin was pushed behind the scenes because of his sexuality and political affiliations, he leaves behind a legacy that helped transform equal rights in the United States.

X González

Gun Control Activist

"There will always be people that hate you, and they're always going to be wrong."

On Valentine's Day, February 14, 2018, a teenager shot and killed seventeen people at Marjory Stoneman Douglas High School in Parkland, Florida. It was one of the deadliest shootings in modern American history. The following day, the *Guardian* reported that there had been 1,624 mass shootings in the US in the 1,870 days prior. These senseless acts of violence had become commonplace in America, and little was done in response to them other than people offering their "thoughts and prayers" while waiting for the next one to occur. But this time was different. This time, the students relentlessly spoke up to push for gun safety laws, and one of those students was eighteen-year-old X González. Days after the shooting at their school, González gave a speech at a federal courthouse in which they put pressure on politicians and the NRA. Within moments, the speech went viral. Shortly after the rally, González and their classmates attended a town hall hosted by CNN, where they stood up to NRA spokesperson, Dana Loesch. González made such an impact at the event that their Twitter account quickly gained more followers than the official NRA account.

The students kept up the pressure by organizing protests, rallies, and speaking with politicians. In addition, X also used their voice by writing op-eds in the *New York Times*, *Teen Vogue*, and *Harper's Bazaar*. In less than a month after the shooting, the students pressured Florida politicians to take action, passing the "Marjory Stoneman Douglas High School Public Safety Act." The law raised the minimum age for buying a gun from eighteen to twenty-one, allocated money to mental health assistance in schools, established waiting periods and background checks, allowed for the arming of some teachers, banned bump stocks, and more. The students then went on to lead the March for Our Lives protest against gun violence, in which more than two million people participated in Washington, DC, and around the world.

González, who is openly bisexual and ran their school's Gay-Straight Alliance for three years, continues to push for meaningful gun legislation in the States and works to prevent the reelection of politicians who take money from the NRA.

Nyle DiMarco

Model, Actor, and Activist

"With sign language, I was able to embrace my own identity as Deaf. I did not let being Deaf define me. Instead, I defined it."

Nyle DiMarco has been breaking down barriers and stereotypes ever since he was thrust into the spotlight when he appeared on the television show *America's Next Top Model* in 2015. DiMarco was the first deaf contestant in the history of the show. Since he uses American Sign Language with facial expressions and body movements, his deafness amplified his natural talent, helping him win the competition. Soon afterward, DiMarco broke down stereotypes again when he became a contestant on *Dancing with the Stars*. Even though he couldn't hear the music, being a visual person, he was able to pick up on small details and cues provided by his dance partner. And while he wasn't the first deaf person to compete on *Dancing with the Stars* (that credit goes to Marlee Matlin), he was the first deaf contestant to win on the show. Many people have the misconception that deaf people can't dance because they can't hear the music, but DiMarco proved them wrong.

Winning television competitions has given DiMarco a giant platform to advocate and raise awareness for issues relating to the deaf community. He created the Nyle DiMarco Foundation, a 501(c)(3) non-profit organization dedicated to improving the lives of deaf people around the world, with a focus on bilingual education (American Sign Language and English) for deaf children. According to the World Federation of the Deaf, there are seventy million deaf people around the globe, and only about 2 percent of them have access to sign language education. When children do not have early access to language, they can have difficulties in functioning, socializing, communicating with other people, and overall learning. That's why, through his foundation, DiMarco has worked toward ensuring that all deaf children in the United States have access to language before they reach five years of age.

Taking his message global, DiMarco addressed the United Nations in 2018 and helped them mark September 23 as the first International Day of Sign Languages. During his visit, he raised awareness of sign languages and the rights of persons with disabilities all over the world. He also advocated for more countries to recognize sign language as an official language.

In addition to being an inspiration to millions of deaf people, DiMarco is also a role model for people in the LGBTQ+ community. *Attitude* magazine honored him with its 2017 Man of the Year award for being a tireless fighter for equality. DiMarco identifies as genderfluid and lives his life out and proud, encouraging everyone to embrace their own identity in order to thrive.

Cecelia Maria Zarbo Wambach, PhD

Humanitarian and Educator

Cecelia Wambach on the right.

"They all have PTSD. Many of them have seen their parents killed in front of them. The stories are heartbreaking and the kids are magnificent."

When Cecelia Wambach was growing up as the second-oldest child in a family of fourteen children in Pennsylvania, she never dreamed she'd be traveling to Lesbos, Greece, to help refugee children from Syria, Afghanistan, Sudan, and other war-torn countries. She's become an ambassador of compassion. Her bicultural Italian and Bohemian Jewish roots, along with a Catholic education, imbued Dr. Wambach with a calling to use her talents and gifts to create a better world. And the Jewish concept of *Tikkun Olam* spurred her desire to *heal the world*.

A PhD in Math Education from Fordham University led her, eventually, to San Francisco State University, where she started an urban education program in an inner-city school. While serving as both professor and co-principal of John Muir Elementary School, the Muir Alternative Teacher Education program she developed won the CCTC Quality of Education Award for Service to Teachers and Children.

Dr. Wambach, who has been married to her wife for over twenty years and is now a grandmother to four, retired as Professor Emerita. But her calling to help children was strong, and she soon found herself cultivating educational solutions for refugees "stuck" on the Greek Island of Lesbos, fewer than five miles from the Turkish coast. As the founder and Volunteer Director of Refugee Education and Learning International (REAL International), a 501(c)(3), Dr. Wambach brought all of her skills to bear in giving traumatized children creative educational experiences. She also fundraised for the organization, and recruited and trained volunteers.

Collaborating with the Greek non-government organization Together for Better Days, Dr. Wambach and the volunteers at

REAL International have worked to create learning centers for asylum-seeking refugees. They help unaccompanied minors and young adults displaced by war and extreme poverty to learn about topics such as computing, ecology, languages, and humanities.

According to UNICEF (United Nations International Children's Emergency Fund), only 29 percent of the twelve thousand school-age refugee and migrant children ages six to seventeen in Greece received formal education during the 2016–17 school year, and refugee and migrant children have missed an average of two and a half years of school due to conflict and displacement. Dr. Wambach hopes to improve those statistics. Back in the States, she actively recruits volunteers and accompanies them once or twice a year, for months at a time. The safe space of school allows refugees to explore, play, and learn and affords Dr. Wambach yet another opportunity to practice *Tikkun Olam, to repair the world.*

Part 2
BUSINESS

Beth Ford

President and CEO, Land O'Lakes

*"The mission of agriculture is a noble one:
do the work to feed the world."*

Beth Ford is a living example of the American dream. She started small, worked hard, and climbed her way up the corporate ladder, becoming one of the top business executives in the United States. Ford was born in Iowa, and she has seven older brothers and sisters. Her first job as a teenager was de-tasseling corn and cutting out weeds in soybean fields for two dollars an hour. By age fifty-four, she was the first out lesbian CEO of a Fortune 500 company and just one of the twenty-five women CEOs in the same list. Ford got her undergraduate business degree from Iowa State University and her master's degree from Columbia University. She went on to hold senior-level positions at large organizations such as Mobil Corporation, PepsiCo, Scholastic, and Hachette before joining Land O'Lakes in 2011.

Land O'Lakes is a farmer-owned dairy and agriculture company with ten thousand employees working in fifty US states and fifty countries. They have a farm-to-fork view of agriculture, and are focused on the challenge of feeding more people while using less water and less land. During her tenure at Land O'Lakes, Ford was able to get the company to invest in technology and R&D, resulting in more plant-friendly farming techniques. She led them through record performance and growth, and helped the cooperative move beyond its reputation of just selling butter. When Land O'Lakes promoted Ford to CEO in 2018, she had helped the fourteen-billion-dollar co-op become one of the nation's largest food and agriculture cooperatives, ranking number 216 on the Fortune 500. The company's press release welcomed Ford to the new role and detailed her extensive experience. It ended by saying, "Ford and her spouse, Jill Schurtz, have three teenage children and live in Minneapolis." That statement made headlines around the world when people realized a company on the Fortune 500 would finally have an openly lesbian CEO.

In 2018, she was ranked number thirty on Fortune Magazine's "Most Powerful Women in Business List." At a time when a Human Rights Campaign survey has found that nearly half of all American LGBTQ+ workers are in the closet, Ford's rise is impressive. "I made a decision long ago to live an authentic life, and if my being named CEO helps others do the same, that's a wonderful moment."

Rick Welts

Former President and CEO, Golden State Warriors

on right

"I hope that my being here is some recognition for all the people behind the scenes for the sport of basketball that they love."

S tarting his career in 1969 as a ball boy for the Seattle
SuperSonics, Rick Welts spent decades rising through
the ranks to become one of the NBA's top executives, and
eventually one of the most respected executives in the industry.
From 1982 to 1999, Welts worked at the NBA league office in
New York, and eventually became the Executive Vice President
and Chief Marketing Officer of NBA Properties. During
this time, he created the massively successful NBA All-Star
Weekend, in addition to the marketing program for the 1992
Olympics "Dream Team." When America's interest in the sport
soared, Welts was credited with enhancing the league's image
and making basketball the popular sport it is today.

One of his basketball legacies came about when he joined
sports attorney Val Ackerman to create the Women's National
Basketball Association (WNBA). The two were instrumental
in launching the women's professional basketball league
and securing partnerships with some of the biggest sports
advertisers in the world, including Nike, Coca-Cola, and
McDonald's. Together, for their efforts, he and Ackerman
were named BRANDWEEK's '97 Grand Marketers of the year.
Later, Welts became the President and Chief Executive Officer
of the Phoenix Suns, and they won three Division Titles (2005,
2006, and 2007) during his tenure with the team.

But one of his most meaningful moments was in 2011,
when he publicly came out in a front-page story in the *New
York Times*. By doing so, Welts became the first openly gay
executive of a major sports team, and an inspiration to many.
He received awards from GLAAD, GLSEN, and even served as
the celebrity Grand Marshal in the 2015 San Francisco Pride
Parade. He also became an Advisory Board Member for the
You Can Play Project, an organization dedicated to ensuring

the safety and inclusion of all people in sports, including LGBTQ+ athletes, coaches, and fans. Shortly after coming out, and weeks after leaving the Suns, Welts was recruited by the Golden State Warriors. During his time as President and Chief Operating Officer, the Warriors excelled, winning three NBA Championships (2015, 2017, and 2018). Welts has had a remarkable career spanning over forty years, and in 2018, he was inducted into the Naismith Memorial Basketball Hall of Fame. In his acceptance speech, he acknowledged his lifelong love of sports and its power to bring people together. He also thanked his partner, Todd Gage, and said that, even though he has accomplished many things throughout his career, coming out was the most important thing he had ever done.

After nine years together, Welts and Gage were married at the San Francisco City Hall in 2020 with a ceremony officiated by San Francisco Mayor London Breed. He retired from his position with the Warriors shortly after in 2021, but he agreed to stay on as an advisor to the team. After all his success leading the Warriors, it's easy to see why.

Suze Orman

Personal Financial Expert

"People first. Then money. Then things."

For fourteen years, every week, Suze Orman reached three million people with *The Suze Orman Show*, an Emmy Award-winning program about money and personal financial independence. She became America's go-to person for financial advice and, in addition to hosting her own show, made regular appearances on various others including *The View*, *Anderson Cooper 360*, *Good Morning America*, and *Larry King Live*. As the host of one of CNBC's most successful television shows, Orman would take calls from viewers and give them advice on how to fix their financial problems, discussing everything from paying off student loan debt to saving for a mortgage. She educated millions of people on stocks and bonds, and explained how long it would take to pay off their credit cards if they only made the minimum payment. Orman is known for tough love, telling it like it is, and never sugarcoating her message to viewers.

In addition to her television show, Orman is the author of nine consecutive *New York Times* bestsellers. Her books educate readers on how to be smart with money in any situation. She was a longtime contributing editor to *O, The Oprah Magazine* and a regular columnist for *AARP* magazine. She was included in *Forbe's* list of the World's 100 Most Power Women and was twice named to *Time* magazine's list of the World's 100 Most Influential People. While on top of the world, Orman came out in a 2007 interview with the *New York Times*. She said she was in a seven-year relationship with her life partner, K.T. The two were married in 2010 and have since retired to a mansion in the Bahamas. Her advice to you, no matter what your background or challenges are, is: "If you hold on to your goals and dreams, you will get there."

Tim Cook

CEO, Apple

"The sidelines are not where you want to live your life. The world needs you in the arena."

Many people know that Steve Jobs was the co-founder of Apple and the product visionary of the company, but did you know it was a gay man who turned their leading product, the iPhone, into one of the most successful tech products in history? Tim Cook became the CEO of Apple in 2011, and, three years later, became the first openly gay man to run a Fortune 500 company, after coming out of the closet in a *Bloomberg* editorial. As if that wasn't enough, Apple became the first one-trillion-dollar publicly traded US company under his leadership.

Most of Apple's profits have been driven by the iPhone, which tens of millions of Americans use in their everyday lives to make calls, send texts, take pictures, check email, listen to music, post on social media, play games, and more. Cook used the product to take high-tech security features normally only used by businesses and made them available to homes around the world. Ordinary people suddenly had the capability of unlocking their devices using fingerprint technology or by scanning their faces, something that was previously only seen in sci-fi movies. He also revolutionized the way consumers make purchases when Apple rolled out a digital wallet, giving people the ability to replace their credit cards with their phones when making in-person purchases.

In addition to being a leader in the business and technology fields, Cook is also a leader when it comes to social issues, and has a long history of supporting LGBTQ+ equality. In 2013, he wrote an opinion piece in the *Wall Street Journal*, urging the US Senate to pass the Employment Non-Discrimination Act (ENDA), a bill that would ban employment discrimination based on sexual orientation and/or gender identity. In 2015, he pushed even harder for LGBTQ+ equality. He wrote an op-ed in the *Washington Post* against "religious freedom" bills (laws that would legalize discrimination against LGBTQ+ people if done for religious reasons), wrote a statement to the Human Rights Campaign in support of the Equality Act (a bill that would provide protections from discrimination for LGBTQ+ people in employment, housing, credit, education, and other key areas of life), and he even got Apple to file a joint friend-of-the-court brief to the US Supreme Court, urging them to overturn same-sex marriage bans. When the court finally ruled that marriage equality was legal across the country, Cook celebrated by marching in the San Francisco Pride Parade with approximately eight thousand Apple employees.

Cook has also used his platform, and Apple's position of influence in the world, to stand up on other social issues, such as racism, immigration, and climate change. For example, after the 2017 alt-right rally in Charlottesville, Virginia, that left one counterprotester dead and nineteen people injured, Cook pledged one million dollars in donations to both the Southern Poverty Law Center and the Anti-Defamation League. In 2017, Apple joined other companies in filing a joint court brief against Trump's stringent Executive Order on Immigration, which halted entry of all refugees and banned citizens from seven predominantly Muslim nations. The companies all agreed that increased background checks were important, but so was America's commitment to welcoming immigrants. The brief made the claim that "Immigrants do not take jobs away from US citizens—they create them," while pointing out that immigrants or their children founded more than two hundred of the Fortune 500 companies, including Apple. In his role as CEO of the largest tech company in the world, Tim Cook has proved that LGBTQ+ people can be great business leaders. Ironically, even more than his stellar leadership, big heart, and generous financial contributions, Cook's forthright example as the most recognizable gay businessperson in the public eye is likely to have the most far-reaching impact on all people, both queer and straight.

Part 3

THE ARTS

Frida Kahlo

World-Renowned Painter

*"I am not sick. I am broken.
But I'm happy to be alive as long as I can paint."*

Frida Kahlo was born on July 6, 1907, in Coyoacán, Mexico City, Mexico, and her life was an uphill battle from the beginning. She was born with spina bifida (a condition where the spinal column doesn't form properly while in the womb), diagnosed with polio at age six, and was in a horrific bus accident at age eighteen. Throughout her life, she had over thirty operations, but Kahlo was a strong woman whose fortitude and perseverance later shined through her art and inspired many. She went on to become one of the most famous surrealist artists in the world.

Kahlo never planned on becoming an artist. She had been accepted to a prestigious premed program at the age of fifteen and was on track to become a doctor. But in 1927, a horrible accident changed everything. A bus she was riding collided with a trolley, leaving her with a fractured spine, shattered pelvis, and damage to her collarbone, foot, ribs, and shoulder. She was bedridden for months. During her convalescence, Frida Kahlo painted with a mirror, often showing in gory detail, the surgeries and treatments she endured. Kahlo would continue to paint throughout her life, mostly self-portraits and many of them surreal with a sense of anguish.

Kahlo later joined the Mexican Communist Party and was introduced to Diego Rivera, one of the world's greatest muralists, through a mutual connection. In 1929, the two of them married and had a tumultuous relationship filled with multiple affairs, including one between Rivera and Kahlo's beloved sister. Frida Kahlo once said, "There have been two great accidents in my life. One was the trolley and the other was Diego. Diego was by far the worst." The couple divorced in 1939, but they married again the following year while both of them continued having affairs. Kahlo's letters reveal romantic attachments to Georgia O'Keefe, probably the greatest woman painter of her time, and a few movie stars, some of whom she shared with Rivera.

Kahlo's paintings continued to enthrall people around the world, especially after the Louvre purchased *The Frame* in 1939, the first work by a twentieth-century Mexican artist to be purchased by a major international museum. But as her popularity began to increase, her health worsened. In the 1950s, she was diagnosed with gangrene and spent many more months in the hospital, and ultimately part of her right leg was amputated. But she never stopped painting. In fact, she finally had a one-person show in 1953 and even though she was still bedridden from surgery, she refused to miss the opening night. She rode an ambulance to the event and was carried to a bed that was transferred from her home so she could participate in the celebration.

After her death at age forty-seven in 1954, Kahlo became world famous as one of the greatest surrealist painters ever, even though she rejected the label while she was still alive, often saying that she just painted her reality. Rediscovered by feminist artists in the 1970s, Kahlo's fame only grew. She became the first Latin American artist whose painting garnered more than $1 million at an auction when her painting *Diego y yo (Diego and I)* sold for $1.4 million. That same painting broke the record again in 2021 when it sold for $34.9 million, the highest price ever paid for Latin American art.

Frida Kahlo has been honored posthumously numerous times. In 2001, she became the first Hispanic woman to be honored with a US postage stamp, and, in 2018, a street was named after her in San Francisco. In her native city of Coyoacán, a park was named for her, and the Bank of Mexico even released a five hundred peso note with Frida Kahlo on one side and Diego Rivera on the other. It's easy to see that Frida Kahlo truly is a global treasure.

Bill T. Jones

Dancer and Tony Award-Winning Choreographer

"We can get up and do it over again, better."

When it comes to modern dance, Bill T. Jones is one of the most notable choreographers and directors of our time. He was born the tenth of twelve children to migrant potato pickers and studied at Binghamton University, which he attended on a special program for underprivileged students. While there, he studied West African and Afro-Caribbean dance, classical ballet, and modern dance. From there, he went on to become the Artistic Director of New York Live Arts and Artistic Director/Co-Founder of the Bill T. Jones/Arnie Zane Dance Company.

Politics, race, and social issues have often been themes in Jones' work. As a longtime AIDS survivor, HIV and AIDS have frequently been highlighted in his pieces. He choreographed *Absence*, which showcased heartrending performances that expressed his grief following the death of his partner, Arnie Zane, who died of AIDS-related lymphoma. In 1994, he choreographed *Still/Here*, a controversial piece that explored mortality and what it's like to live with a life-threatening medical diagnosis. His work gained national attention, and in that year, he graced the cover of *Time* magazine.

Jones also made a significant mark on the Broadway stage. In 2007, he won the Tony Award for Best Choreography for the musical, *Spring Awakening*, the story of a nineteenth-century German schoolgirl coming of age and the collective rebellion of German teens in an era of repression and structure. In 2010, he again won the Tony Award for Best Choreography, this time for *FELA!*, a musical based on the life of Fela Kuti, the Afrobeat musician and activist who was jailed numerous times in his young life and was severely beaten after speaking out against the Nigerian army. Jones has received prestigious honors for his provocative work that spans decades. He was inducted into the American Academy of Arts and Sciences in 2009, and was a Kennedy Center Honoree in 2010. He was recognized as Officier de l'Ordre des Arts et des Lettres by the French government, and was even chosen for the National Medal of Arts by President Obama in 2013. When it comes to performance arts, Bill T. Jones has definitely left his mark.

Jin Xing

Award-Winning Dancer, Talk Show Host, and Entertainer

"I don't want to change the world, but I also don't want the world to change me too much. I just want to be myself."

An army colonel and a prima ballerina may seem like polar opposites, but both of them adequately describe Jin Xing. Born in Shenyang, Liaoning, China, in 1967, Xing joined the People's Liberation Army performance troupe when she was only nine years old. In the military, she spent part of her time studying dance and performance arts while, at other times, learning how to use bombs, grenades, and machine guns. Though the two disciplines don't seem to go together, Xing credits much of her success in her professional life to the military discipline she learned while serving in the army. Xing won her first national dance competition at age seventeen and became one of the most celebrated dancers in China. This led her to apply for, and win, a scholarship to study modern dance in America. After critical acclaim in the States, she performed all over Europe before returning home to China.

Her time spent traveling the world gave her the opportunity to reflect on who she was as a person. From an early age, Xing knew she was female, and at age twenty-eight, she decided it was finally time to transition. Since China is such a conservative country, it was risky to be one of the first citizens to have gender confirmation surgery. Acceptance was slow at first, but society eventually embraced Xing. She was the first transgender person to be officially recognized by the Chinese government, and has since been able to adopt three children and get married.

In addition, she has risen to become one of China's most popular entertainment personalities. Along with forming the Beijing Modern Dance Company and the Jin Xing Dance Theater, Xing became a popular judge on the local version of *So You Think You Can Dance*. Audiences loved her so much that she wound up getting the opportunity to host some of

China's most popular TV shows, including her own variety/
chat program called *The Jin Xing Show*, which had an estimated
one hundred million viewers every week, and a show called
Chinese Dating with the Parents, where parents decide who their
sons can date. While the latter may sound a bit controversial,
Xing says the show depicts real life in China, where parents
still play a major role in whom their children marry. Xing has
done many things in her life. She's been a military colonel,
a choreographer, a prima ballerina, a competition judge, a
television host, and more, but one thing has always remained
consistent. Xing commands attention and stands out in a
crowd. Above all, she's an entertainer.

Part 4

FILM & TELEVISION

RuPaul

Award-Winning Entertainer and the World's Most Famous Drag Queen

"We're all born naked and the rest is drag."

At 6'4" tall and wearing elaborate wigs, makeup, and gowns, RuPaul stands out. He started performing drag in the underground scene in Atlanta, Georgia, before moving to New York. But RuPaul had something unique that set him apart and propelled him into international fame: star quality. He's a *New York Times* bestselling author, an Emmy Award-winning television host, and a musician with multiple *Billboard* charting albums. He's often referred to as the "Queen of Drag" and, commercially, he's the most successful drag queen in the world. But more than that, he brought the art of drag into homes around the world.

RuPaul released a dance-pop album, *Supermodel of the World*, in 1993, and the popularity of the upbeat single, "Supermodel (You Better Work)," led to movie roles, an autobiography, and a contract with M.A.C. Cosmetics, making RuPaul the first drag queen to become a spokesmodel for a major cosmetics company. He followed up that venture with a talk show, *The RuPaul Show*, which was the first national television program in the US to have an openly gay host and the first national talk show to be hosted by a drag queen. The program ran for two years and had guest appearances by Cher, Cyndi Lauper, Diana Ross, Lil Kim, and many other celebrities.

As an entertainer, RuPaul has appeared in numerous films and television shows, but he's probably best known for being the host and executive producer of *RuPaul's Drag Race*, a reality show where contestants do various challenges and compete to become "America's next drag superstar." The show premiered in 2009 and, as of 2024, has aired for sixteen seasons with no signs of slowing down. There have been numerous spinoffs, including *RuPaul's Drag U*, *RuPaul's Drag Race All Stars*, and *RuPaul's Celebrity Drag Race*. As of 2023, the show has received a total of seventy-one Emmy nominations and twenty-nine wins. RuPaul has a total of fourteen Emmy awards himself, making him the most-decorated Black artist in Emmy history. *Drag Race* is credited for de-mystifying the art of drag and making it more accessible by bringing it into homes around the world.

Consistently throughout his career, RuPaul has also used his platform to raise money and awareness for various causes. He helped raise money to support people living with HIV/ AIDS and is an active supporter of voter registration, doing announcements for National Voter Registration Day and ending episodes of Drag Race with queens holding signs that encourage people to vote. RuPaul also partnered with World of Wonder, MTV, and the ACLU to create the Drag Defense Fund in order to defeat drag ban laws and bring attention to the increasing number of anti-LGBTQ+ attacks sweeping the nation.

As an author, RuPaul has released four books, including the 2024 *New York Times* bestseller, *The House of Hidden Meanings*, and, as of 2023, he has released a total of sixteen albums as a recording artist. He's the cohost for the podcast, *What's the Tee?* with Michelle Visage on iTunes, and he's also the host for DragCon, the world's largest in-person celebration of drag culture. RuPaul is not just a drag queen. He's an actor, singer, producer, writer, activist, and television personality. He's a well-rounded entertainer who changed the entertainment industry and made it more inclusive.

Hannah Gadsby

Emmy and Peabody Award-Winning Comedian, Writer, and Actor

"The future can be joyful and terrifying in equal measure. But when you're trapped in trauma, you're unable to think about the future."

B orn the youngest of five children in Tasmania, Australia, in 1978, Hannah Gadsby broke normal comedy rules when they shared their horror stories of being sexually abused as a child, beat up at a bus stop for being gender nonconforming, and raped as a young adult. On their Netflix televised comedy show, *Nanette*, Gadsby explored dark material including homophobia, xenophobia, sexism, and gendered violence. Their work captured the zeitgeist in Australia when an epidemic of gender-based violence was declared a "national crisis" by the federal government in 2015. For this groundbreaking work, Gadsby became an international sensation, winning numerous awards including a Primetime Emmy Award for Outstanding Writing in 2018 and a Peabody Award for Entertainment in 2019.

At age thirty-nine, Gadsby, who identifies as genderqueer, was diagnosed with autism and ADHD. As a neurodiverse person in a world of neurotypical adults, Gadsby finally realized that their inability to "read" people, communicate their feelings, and understand others easily was not their fault. Gadsby is open about their diagnosis and has spent a great deal of time candidly talking about it in their second comedy special, *Douglas*. In an interview with ABC News Australia, they said it would be nice if people on the spectrum who watched *Douglas* could "recognize something of themselves in it and maybe give them a bit more confidence to sort of have pride in their identity and the way they think about the world." Gadsby has also spoken about their experience with autism and ADHD in numerous interviews, helping people get a better understanding of what it's like for neurodiverse people.

In 2021, Gadsby married Jenney Shamash who produced Gadsby's off-Broadway comedy show, *Nanette*. That same year, they were awarded an honorary doctorate of letters from the University of Tasmania. In their address to graduates, they asked the question, "Who do you want to be?" After several repetitions, they answered the question for themselves: to "be kind."

Gadsby also became a *New York Times* bestselling author in 2022 with the publication of *Ten Steps to Nanette: A Memoir Situation*. The book was critically acclaimed and received starred reviews from the *Library Journal* and *Publishers Weekly*.

Hannah Gadsby stands out from other comedians because of their unique ability to talk about difficult topics in a matter-of-fact way with humor and grace. This has resulted in them winning over the world with their charm.

Ariana DeBose

Academy Award-Winning Actress

"To anybody who's ever questioned your identity or who found yourself in the gray spaces, I promise you this: 'There is, indeed, a place for us.' "

Ariana DeBose was born on January 25, 1991, in Wilmington, North Carolina, and her mother, Gina DeBose likes to tell people, "she came out dancing." At the age of three, DeBose started taking dance lessons in ballet, tap, and jazz. When she was eighteen years old, she competed on the reality TV show, *So You Think You Can Dance*, making it into the top twenty before being eliminated. Despite being discouraged by the rejection, she turned to musical theater. There, she appeared in shows like *Hairspray*; *Bring It On: The Musical*; *Motown: The Musical*; *Pippin*; *A Bronx Tale*; *Summer: The Donna Summer Musical* (for which she received a Tony nomination); and the sensational hit, *Hamilton*. But her big break was starring in the movie remake of *West Side Story*.

When DeBose first heard about Steven Spielberg's *West Side Story*, she was reluctant to audition for the role of Anita because she didn't think she fit Hollywood's stereotype of what it meant to be Latina. Her mother is white, her father is Puerto Rican, she has African-American lineage, and she's also part-Italian. But she *did* audition, and she got the part. It turned out to be the role of a lifetime. DeBose won an Academy Award for Best Supporting Actress in 2022 making her the first Afro-Latina, the first openly queer actor of color, and the first openly queer woman to win an Oscar. She also won a BAFTA, a Critics' Choice Award, a Golden Globe, and a SAG Award for that role. DeBose has appeared in other films as well, including Netflix's *The Prom* (along with Meryl Streep, Kerry Washington, and James Corden) and Apple Original Films' *Argylle* (alongside Dua Lipa, Henry Cavill, and Samuel L. Jackson). She even voiced the main character, Asha, in Disney's animated film, *Wish*.

DeBose is a versatile performer, and her triple threat talents—dancer, singer, and actor—led her to be chosen as host of the Tony Awards three years in a row: 2022, 2023, and 2024. She was also listed as one of *Time* magazine's 100 most influential people.

Beyond her own personal success, alongside her *Prom* co-star, JoAnn Pellman, DeBose established the Unruly Hearts Initiative, a nonprofit, concentrating on finding housing, mental health access, mentorship, and educational opportunities for queer youth. She is committed to making positive change both on and off the screen.

Daniela Vega

Award-Winning Actress

"Soy muy auténtica." ("I'm the real deal.")

B orn in Santiago in 1989, Chilean native Daniela Vega found it difficult to find work after transitioning. So much so that she started getting depressed. But everything started looking up when someone she knew asked her to be part of a makeup team for a theater production, marking the beginning of Vega's journey to success. Through a friend, Vega began sitting in on courses at university. She sang and tried out for stage roles, further developing her love of the performing arts. Eventually, she acted in a solo show about her transition, *La Mujer Mariposa* (*The Butterfly Woman*), which ran for eight years in Santiago. After her screen debut in the 2015 Chilean film *La Visita*, Vega ultimately landed the role of a lifetime.

Director Sebastián Lelio initially approached Vega to be a culture consultant for his film, *Una Mujer Fantástica*, (*A Fantastic Woman*), but after working with her for a while, he felt she would be perfect for the starring role. It's common to cast cisgender actors in transgender roles (Jeffrey Tambor in *Transparent*, Felicity Huffman in *Transamerica*, Eddie Redmayne in *The Danish Girl*, Hilary Swank in *Boys Don't Cry*, and Jared Leto in *Dallas Buyers Club*), but rare to cast transgender actors in transgender roles. When Lelio cast Vega as the lead in his movie, they helped change that. Vega's mezzo-soprano singing voice enabled her to sing her own songs in the movie. For her searing performance, she won Chile's prestigious honor, the Caleuche Acting Award for Best Actress, and the Best Actress Award at the Palm Springs International Film Festival, for her portrayal of Marina Vidal, a transgender woman in mourning after the untimely death of her boyfriend. In 2018, Daniela Vega made history by becoming the first openly transgender woman to present at the Oscars, and *A Fantastic Woman* also made history when it became the first Oscar winner to feature a transgender storyline with an openly trans person playing the lead role. *A Fantastic Woman* was also the first Chilean movie to win an Academy Award for Best Foreign Film, making Vega's home country proud.

Time magazine named Vega one of the World's 100 Most Influential People, and Michelle Bachelet, the former President of Chile, praised Vega and the rest of the team who worked on the film. Bachelet posted on X (formerly Twitter):

"My biggest compliments to @slelio, @danivega @tengochicle and the whole team #UnaMujerFantástica! The prize, which fills us with pride, not only recognizes a film of great quality, but a history of respect for the diversity that makes us good as a country. #Oscars."

Robin Roberts

Award-Winning News Anchor

"Optimism is a muscle—it gets stronger with use."

Robin Roberts graduated with a Bachelor of Arts degree in Communications from Southern Louisiana University. Combining her education and love of sports, she became a sports reporter for a local television station in Mississippi. As she advanced in her career and became a news anchor, her compassion, transparency, and ability to connect with viewers led her to being voted the "Most Trusted Person on Television" by a 2013 *Reader's Digest* poll. In 1995, Roberts began contributing to *Good Morning America*, and ten years later, ABC hired her as a full-time co-anchor on the show. As a co-anchor, she helped the broadcast become the number-one morning show on television, winning five Emmy Awards and a People's Choice Award. Roberts was also honored with the Walter Cronkite Award for Excellence in Journalism and the George Foster Peabody Award. She was even inducted into the Broadcasting & Cable Hall of Fame. In 2018, she received the Lifetime Achievement Award from the Radio Television Digital News Foundation.

One of the things that sets Roberts apart from so many others in the industry is her ability to wear her heart on her sleeve and emotionally empathize with her viewers. When Hurricane Katrina hit the Gulf Coast of the United States, she was temporarily unable to contact family members, leaving her to wonder if they had survived. Thankfully, they had, but much of her hometown of Pass Christian, Mississippi, was destroyed, including her high school. Because she was personally impacted, when Roberts reported on the storm, viewers affected by the disaster were able to relate to her in a unique way.

In 2012, Roberts experienced a life-changing moment. On the day she was granted an interview with President Barack

Obama about same-sex marriage, Roberts found out she had myelodysplastic syndrome (MDS), a rare disease that attacks a person's blood and bone marrow. Her condition was life-threatening and would require a bone marrow transplant. Stunned by the news, she decided to go ahead with the groundbreaking interview, in which the president reversed his earlier position and endorsed same-sex marriage. That interview probably did more to change hearts and minds than any other. Soon afterward, Roberts decided to go public with the news of her disease and announced on *GMA* that she would be taking a leave of absence to undergo chemotherapy, blood tests, and isolation in preparation for and recovery from a bone marrow transplant. Once again, the viewers connected with Roberts. Her announcement on the show resulted in an 1,800-percent spike in donor registration with the National Marrow Donor Program Match Registry. While going through treatment, she allowed her network to document her journey and build a public service campaign in an effort to raise awareness of the rare disease. Thankfully, Roberts made a full recovery, and came back stronger than ever. It's no wonder she was voted the "Most Trusted Person on Television." She bares her soul and reveals the most intimate moments of her life in order to help other people.

Chris Nee

Emmy Award-Winning Writer and Producer

*"It's so powerful to show representation
of somebody who's not usually on TV."*

C hris Nee began her career as an associate producer at Sesame Street International, and went on to create groundbreaking television show characters for Disney. Some of her earlier writing credits include *Blue's Clues, American Dragon: Jake Long, Johnny and the Sprites, Higglytown Heroes, The Backyardigans, Wonder Pets!,* and *Henry Hugglemonster.* Nee wound up spending a lot of time in the doctor's office while her two-year-old son was being treated for asthma, and it was then that she realized nobody had done a show to help make doctor visits less scary for kids. She came up with an idea for an animated series in which a little girl was a doctor for stuffed animals and broken toys. That show became Disney Junior's *Doc McStuffins,* and with a young, African-American girl interested in science as the main character, it inspired children around the world. The show became an instant hit, as the series premiere attracted 1.08 million viewers ages two to five, prompting *AdWeek* to call the show a "ratings juggernaut." That interest spilled into the toy industry as well. In 2013, *Doc McStuffins* merchandise generated about five hundred million dollars in sales, and according to the *New York Times*, industry experts said that the toys seemed to be "setting a record as the best-selling toy line based on an African-American character."

The show was such a cultural phenomenon that even First Lady Michelle Obama guest-starred in one of the episodes. Following up on the success of *Doc McStuffins,* Nee became Executive Producer on another Disney Junior show called *Vampirina,* based on the *Vampirina Ballerina* book series by Anne Marie Pace. The show is about a young vampire who has to learn how to fit in and make new friends in the human world after moving with her family from Transylvania to Pennsylvania. The show was another instant hit. With an Emmy Award, a Peabody Award, and a Humanitas Prize under her belt, Chris Nee is a powerhouse in the children's television industry, creating shows that inspire young kids and allow them to see themselves represented in the shows they watch.

Sir Ian McKellen

Global Award-Winning Actor

"I've never met a gay person who regretted coming out—including myself. Life at last begins to make sense, when you are open and honest."

In Hollywood, many LGBTQ+ actors stay in the closet because they fear they'll lose fans and/or acting jobs, but Sir Ian McKellen is an example of how one doesn't need to hide who they are in order to have a successful career as an actor. He made his professional debut on stage in *A Man for All Seasons* at the Belgrade Theater in 1961, and went on to star in some of the biggest blockbuster movie franchises in the world. McKellen has played numerous roles over the last few decades, but his most notable film roles include James Whale in *Gods and Monsters*, Magneto in the *X-Men* films, Gandalf in *The Lord of the Rings* and *The Hobbit* trilogies, Sir Leigh Teabing in *The Da Vinci Code*, Sherlock Holmes in *Mr. Holmes*, and Cogsworth in Disney's live-action version of *Beauty and the Beast*. He has won numerous awards including six Olivier Awards, a Critics' Choice Movie Award, a Golden Globe Award, a Saturn Award, a Screen Actors Guild Award, and a Tony Award. During a 1988 interview with BBC Radio 3, McKellen publicly came out as a gay man while speaking out against Section 28, a bill that banned the promotion of homosexuality in the UK and made it illegal to discuss homosexuality in schools in a positive way. He continued speaking out for equality, and later that year, with other activists, he helped found Stonewall, an LGBTQ+ charity in the UK, named after the riots in New York.

In addition to helping the LGBTQ+ community, McKellen has also done charity work to raise money for earthquake victims, to support the arts, to end homelessness, to help the elderly, to raise awareness for prostate cancer, and much more. He was even knighted by Queen Elizabeth II for his service to the performing arts. It's safe to say that McKellen is more than just an actor. He's a successful actor who has helped make the world a better place.

Margaret Cho

Actress and Award-Winning Comedian

"The power of visibility can never be underestimated."

Born and raised in San Francisco, Margaret Cho, who is openly bisexual, grew up around an eclectic group of people from all walks of life, and because of this, she is able to connect with those who feel marginalized in society. She uses this to her benefit in her stand-up routines, speaking out against racism, sexism, and homophobia. Cho has fought long and hard to be legitimately recognized in an industry dominated by straight white men. Over the course of her career, people criticized her looks and characteristics, calling her too fat and too Asian, but she never let that stop her. When people tried to knock her down, she came back stronger and better than ever, like a phoenix rising from the ashes.

When she was sixteen years old, Cho started her career at a comedy club above a bookstore run by her parents. The unfiltered comedian got her big break in 1991, when she won a comedy competition, the first prize being an opportunity to open for Jerry Seinfeld. Her fan base continued to grow, and in 1994, she won the American Comedy Award for Funniest Female Stand-Up Comic. Cho's success led to her starring in her own TV show, *All-American Girl*, a sitcom in which she played a rebellious teenager in a traditional Korean-American family. The show took a toll on her, though, with producers telling her she was "too Asian" at times and "not Asian enough" at others. They even had the gall to hire a coach so she could learn how to be "more Asian." Cho was also criticized by producers about her weight, leading her to go on a crash diet and lose thirty pounds in just two weeks. The rapid weight loss was unhealthy and resulted in years of serious kidney problems.

Cho turned to drugs and alcohol when the show was canceled. After sobering up, she wrote about the struggles she had faced while filming *All-American Girl*, and turned it into an autobiography and a one-woman comedy show called *I'm the One That I Want*. Her material dealt with issues like race, weight, body image, eating disorders, and substance abuse. The show was a hit, and was released as a concert film the following year.

Cho would later go on to appear in numerous comedy specials, movies, and television shows, including a guest appearance on *30 Rock*, where her performance earned her an Emmy nomination. In 2017, *Rolling Stone* named her one of the "50 Best Stand-Up Comics of All Time."

When she's not making people laugh, Cho fights racism, sexism, homophobia, homelessness, and more. She has performed at rallies for equal rights, and even done pop-up charity performances on street corners to help the homeless. On April 30, 2008, San Francisco Mayor Gavin Newsom officially declared it Margaret Cho Day.

Margaret Cho is fighting the good fight, and has inspired marginalized communities along the way. Through her activism and comedy, she has proven that you can't keep a good girl down.

The Wachowskis

Award-Winning Directors, Producers, and Writers

Lilly

Lana

"The way a film can change over the generations… The movie changes, because we change as individuals."

–Lilly Wachowski

"I couldn't find anyone like me in the world and it felt like my dreams were foreclosed simply because my gender was less typical than others."

–Lana Wachowski

Lana and Lilly Wachowski are Hollywood juggernauts. They made their directorial debut in 1996 with *Bound*, a movie that is believed to be the first mainstream Hollywood film to put a lesbian relationship front and center without making it the main point of the story. After their success with *Bound*, they went on to create one of the most critically acclaimed sci-fi movies ever made. The Wachowskis wrote and directed the blockbuster phenomenon, *The Matrix*. The movie is probably best known for popularizing a visual effect known as "bullet time," in which high-speed actions (such as flying bullets) occur in slow motion while the camera's viewpoint moves through the scene at normal speed. *The Matrix* won numerous awards including four Academy Awards, two BAFTA Awards, three MTV Movie Awards, and two Saturn Awards. The movie was so successful, it spawned two sequels, and even expanded into comic books, video games, and animated short films. Because of the its significant cultural, artistic, and historic achievements, *The Matrix* was selected for preservation in the National Film Registry of the Library of Congress. After completing the *Matrix* trilogy, the Wachowskis went on to produce and write the film adaptation of Alan Moore's graphic novel *V for Vendetta*. They also wrote, directed, and produced *Speed Racer*, *Cloud Atlas*, and *Jupiter Ascending* before writing and directing the Emmy-nominated Netflix series, *Sense8*.

Lana made global headlines when she became the first major Hollywood director to publicly come out as transgender. Her sister, Lilly, also publicly came out as a transgender woman a few years later. The siblings, who have worked side by side throughout their careers, have also been each other's support system along the way, and by living their lives authentically, they became role models for many people around the world.

Part 5

GOVERNMENT & MILITARY

Harvey Milk

One of the First Openly Gay Elected Officials in the Country

*"If a bullet should enter my brain,
let that bullet destroy every closet door."*

Born on May 22, 1930, in New York, Harvey Milk grew up in a middle-class Jewish family on Long Island. After graduating from the New York State College for Teachers, he enlisted in the US Navy in 1951, but he was forced to resign a few years later. He received an "other than honorable" discharge after being officially questioned about his sexual orientation. Despite that discharge, Milk would go on to become one of the most iconic figures in LGBTQ+ history, and, in an attempt to amend their wrongs, the US Navy did an about-face and even named a ship after him.

In 1972, at the age of forty-two, Milk moved to San Francisco and opened a camera store on Castro Street right in the middle of the city's LGBTQ+ community. He got involved in local politics and decided to run for the San Francisco Board of Supervisors. He lost that election, and the two after that, but he learned from his mistakes and continued to press on. On his fourth try, Harvey Milk won and was elected to the San Francisco Board of Supervisors in 1977, becoming the first openly gay elected official in the state of California, and one of the first openly gay elected officials in the country.

Milk was known for being an advocate for all people, not just those in the LGBTQ+ community. He continuously looked for common ground when working on the issues and focused on intersectionality. He supported things like affordable housing, childcare, safer neighborhoods, establishing day care centers for working mothers, improving library services, and much more.

But the issue that brought Harvey Milk into national prominence was his active role in helping to defeat California's Proposition 6 (also known as the Briggs Initiative because it was sponsored by the conservative state legislator, John Briggs). The initiative would have mandated firing teachers and school officials in California's public schools if they were gay or did anything that was considered to be "advocating, soliciting, imposing, encouraging, or promoting of private or public homosexual activity." Milk organized and collaborated with other groups across the state to call out the lies being told about the LGBTQ+ community and to rally support for defeating the Briggs Initiative. Milk even debated John Briggs on television. Those actions garnered national attention and cemented Milk's place in history when the proposition was defeated 58 percent to 42 percent.

Unfortunately, Harvey Milk's career was tragically cut short when he and San Francisco Mayor George Moscone were both assassinated by his colleague, Supervisor Dan White, nearly a year after taking office. Milk's life may have been cut short, but his legacy lives on. There have been numerous biographies written about him, Academy Award-winning films, and even an opera. He has been memorialized with a statue in the rotunda of SF City Hall and President Barack Obama posthumously awarded him the Presidential Medal of Freedom in 2009. The US Postal Service issued a Forever Stamp honoring him in 2014 and a terminal was named after him at the San Francisco airport. As for the military, lesbian, gay, and bisexual people have been able to serve openly since 2011 after the repeal of "Don't Ask, Don't Tell" in 2010. In an attempt to make amends for the "other than honorable" discharge they gave him, the US Navy christened and launched the USNS Harvey Milk in 2021. It's safe to say that Harvey Milk's mark on the world will never be forgotten.

Justice Mary Yu

Washington State Supreme Court Justice

*"I believe different perspectives make our court
better. The more robust the debate,
the better our decisions."*

M ary Yu was born in Chicago, IL, and grew up in a
working-class family. Her parents were both immigrants
(her father from China and her mother from Mexico) who met
while working in a factory. Family was important to them. Her
parents taught her how to be independent and speak up for
herself. They also taught her the importance of hard work and
a good education. And all of those values instilled in her from
an early age helped her forge a path to becoming a justice in the
highest court in the state of Washington.

Yu started her career by getting her BA from Dominican
University and her master's in religious studies from
Mundelein College of Loyola University in Chicago. But
before obtaining her JD from the University of Notre Dame
Law School, she worked in the Peace and Justice Office for the
Archdiocese of Chicago and eventually became the director.
Yu spent her time in the Peace and Justice Office promoting
human dignity and examining racial justice. She advocated
that all people have a right to jobs, healthcare, and housing. It
was there that she solidified her beliefs that people could make
a difference as individuals and collectively. She was drawn to
law school because she saw it as another tool to advance and
promote the common good, especially in the realm of social
and economic justice.

In 2000, Yu was appointed to the King County Superior Court
where she spent fourteen years presiding over a wide variety
of criminal, civil, and juvenile cases. She also presided over
adoptions and other family law matters. Justice Yu was proud
of all her work during this time, but she was especially proud
of the moment where she officiated King County's first same-
sex wedding. In fact, many people around the country were
also interested in this historic moment because the judge had

the perfect name for officiating a wedding: Judge Mary Yu. Her perfectly fitting name became a news story within itself, appearing in *The Stranger* and *Jimmy Kimmel Live!*

Justice Yu has received numerous awards throughout her career, including the Loren Miller Bar Association Lifetime Achievement Award, the Latina/o Bar Association of Washington CZ Smith Trailblazer Award, the Voice of Social Justice Award from the Greater Seattle Business Association, the Daniel K. Inouye Trailblazer Award from the National Asian Pacific American Bar Association, and the Luminary Award at Seattle Women's Pride in 2016.

When she was appointed to the Washington Supreme Court by Gov. Jay Inslee on May 16, 2014, Justice Yu made history by becoming the first Asian, the first Latina, and the first member of the LGBTQ+ community to serve on the Washington Supreme Court. She is a trailblazer, bringing a unique perspective to her judicial responsibilities and allowing her to interpret the law in a manner that promotes equality, protects civil liberties, and ensures equal justice under the law for all.

Pete Buttigieg

US Department of Transportation Secretary and the First Openly Gay Person Confirmed to Serve in a US President's Cabinet

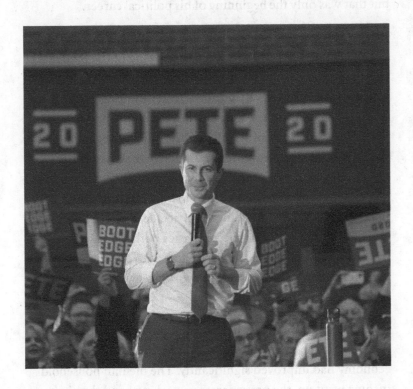

"To love a country, as to love a person,
is to love a flawed and exquisite creation..."

–Trust: America's Best Chance

Pete Buttigieg was born in South Bend, Indiana, on January 19, 1982. After college, he worked on various different political campaigns and soon became a rising star within the Democratic Party. At the age of twenty-nine, he was elected mayor of South Bend, making him the youngest mayor of a city with a population of a hundred thousand in the United States at the time. He revolutionized the deteriorating city during his tenure, but that was only the beginning of his political career.

Before Buttigieg became mayor, South Bend was on a steady decline dating back to 1963 when the closing of the Studebaker car factory resulted in seven thousand people losing their jobs. The population of the city declined thirty thousand from 1960 to 2010 and many of the houses left were empty and rundown. When Buttigieg took office in 2012, he quickly began to turn that around. He implemented an initiative that focused on identifying rundown properties that were vacant or abandoned and either repaired or demolished them. He also championed the creation of the Renaissance District, destined to become one of the largest mixed-use complexes in the Midwest, by transforming the Studebaker factory into a technology complex, a conference center, co-working spaces, retail, and residential condos.

By 2015, South Bend saw its largest population growth in over twenty years and by the time he left office in 2020, the local economy had improved significantly. The median household income went up, the poverty rate went down, and the city's unemployment rate dropped by 8 percent. His efforts even helped South Bend achieve a Gold Rating from SolSmart for advancing solar energy growth.

In 2019, Buttigieg threw his hat in the ring to run for president. While many take the path from Congress to the White House, Buttigieg argued that being mayor of a Midwestern industrial city was the perfect background for tackling things like infrastructure problems, the economy, and the bread-and-butter issues that impact everyday Americans. He also believed his time deployed to Afghanistan put him in a unique position to understand global issues and support fellow American veterans.

Buttigieg stood out from other Democratic candidates because of his willingness to appear on conservative media outlets like Fox News to talk about the issues, and he had an ability to deliver quick counter attacks with a cool and calm demeanor, appealing to people on both sides of the aisle. He also stood out because he was an openly gay man and his husband, Chasten, stood by his side throughout his entire campaign. Buttigieg wound up winning the Iowa Caucuses, becoming the first openly LGBTQ+ person in history to win a presidential primary.

While Buttigieg won Iowa, he placed second in New Hampshire and third in Nevada. He eventually dropped out of the race which was ultimately won by Joe Biden. Buttigieg may have lost the presidency, but he won the trust of President Biden who nominated him to be the Transportation Secretary. Buttigieg was confirmed, making him the first openly gay Cabinet secretary in US history and the youngest person to ever serve as Secretary of Transportation.

Jóhanna Sigurðardóttir

Iceland's First Female Prime Minister and the World's First Openly LGBTQ+ Head of Government

"A society that does not use the intellectual power of its female population fully is not a wise society."

Jóhanna Sigurðardóttir was born in 1942 in Reykjavik, Iceland's capital and largest city. She was elected to Iceland's parliament in 1978 and became the Minister of Social Affairs and Social Security in 1987.

After losing an internal election for the leadership of the Social Democratic Party in 1994, she went on to form her own party, National Awakening. It eventually merged with the Social Democratic Party, the People's Alliance, and the Women's List to form the Social Democratic Alliance.

On February 1, 2009, Jóhanna Sigurðardóttir made history by becoming Iceland's first female prime minister and the world's first openly LGBTQ+ head of government. She was also the country's longest-serving Member of Parliament during her time in office.

When Sigurðardóttir took over as PM, Iceland had just experienced the worst financial disaster in its history. She is widely credited with restoring the economy and bringing back prosperity to the island nation by bolstering tourism and implementing stronger oversight measures in the banking industry. She exemplified Iceland's values of openness, fairness, and social responsibility.

When Iceland legalized marriage equality in 2010, Sigurðardóttir married author and playwright, Jónína Leósdóttir, making them one of the first same-sex couples to marry in the country. They had been in a civil union since 2002.

Sigurðardóttir helped bring Iceland out of a grave financial crisis, crediting her success to getting more women in government roles, thus making the administration more gender-balanced and creating a working government with a shared power structure. It's no wonder that, in the year Sigurðardóttir became prime minister, Iceland ranked number one on the World Economic Forum's annual Global Gender Gap Index, a report that measures equity in education, employment, politics, and health. *Forbes* also listed Sigurðardóttir as one of the 100 Most Powerful Women in the world that year, coming in at number seventy-five.

Leo Varadkar, MD

First Openly Gay Prime Minister of Ireland

*"Politicians should trust people with the truth.
Very often, we don't do that."*

B orn in Ireland in 1979, Leo Varadkar is the son of an Indian doctor and an Irish nurse. In 2017, when he was only thirty-eight years old, he was elected Taoiseach (Irish prime minister), becoming the youngest person to hold that position. He also became the first Irish government leader of an ethnic minority background, the first openly gay Irish government minister, and the world's fourth openly gay head of government in modern times, joining Luxembourg Prime Minister Xavier, former Belgian Prime Minister Elio Di Rupo, and former Icelandic Prime Minister Jóhanna Sigurðardóttir.

Before rising to Taoiseach, Varadkar was Minister of Transport, Tourism, and Sport, and led one of the most successful tourism initiatives in Irish History. "The Gathering," was a staging of five thousand events aimed at attracting members of the Irish diaspora, including the thirty-five million in the US alone, and other visitors to Ireland, a country of five million. During Varadkar's tenure, the number of international visitors to Ireland increased by one million per year.

Varadkar publicly came out as a gay man a few months before Ireland voted on a referendum to define marriage as a legal union between two people regardless of sex, and he became a champion for the cause. During this time, he held the position of Minister for Health, and his high-profile role helped put a human face to the matter. He went on to eloquently defend marriage equality in the Dáil Éireann (Ireland's equivalent of Parliament or Congress), saying, "We believe in marriage as an institution, and so we believe equal marriage makes it stronger and makes society stronger too." When Election Day arrived, 62 percent of voters cast their ballots in favor of marriage equality, and Ireland became the first country in the world to approve same-sex marriage by popular vote.

One of Varadkar's first acts as Taoiseach was to announce a referendum to repeal Ireland's Eighth Amendment, a law that gave "the unborn" the same rights as mothers, and thus effectively banned almost all abortions. Varadkar put his support behind the repeal, and on May 25, 2018, with voter turnout at a near-historic high, the Irish people voted 66.4 percent in favor of removing the ban from the Constitution.

Even though Ireland has long been considered one of Europe's most socially conservative countries, Varadkar has helped liberalize policy on some of their key social issues. He represents a new wave of Irish politics, attempting to ensure economic prosperity, social equality, and health, while holding firm to the "law and order" tenets of the Fine Gail party.

Eric Fanning

Former Secretary of the United States Army

"America's diversity is our army's strength."

E ric Fanning became the first openly gay Secretary of the Army (and the highest-ranking openly LGBTQ+ official ever employed at the Pentagon) when President Obama appointed him on May 18, 2016. In this role, he was responsible for all matters relating to the United States Army, including recruiting, training, personnel, reserve affairs, installations, environmental issues, weapons systems, equipment acquisition, communications, and financial management.

Fanning came from a military family, and growing up, he thought about following in their footsteps and signing up for the armed forces too, but gay people were not allowed to serve in the military and he didn't want to serve in silence. Instead, he took on civilian roles and never actually *served* in the military himself. So how did he become the Secretary of the Army if he never actually served? For separation-of-powers reasons, the United States has civilian control of the military.

The Army is not the only branch of the military that Fanning worked with. In total, Fanning held high-level civilian jobs in three branches of the military, and prior to becoming the Secretary of the Army, he also held positions as Deputy Under Secretary of the Navy, Acting Secretary of the Air Force, and Chief of Staff to the Secretary of Defense.

Fanning felt that being gay gave him a perspective that helped bring a focus to inclusivity and diversity in the army. He believed diversity was an asset, and that the army would be stronger if it looked like society. Because of this, he implemented policies to help the army reflect that belief. During his tenure, he issued grooming and dress waivers to

Sikhs and Muslims for religious reasons, and even helped the Pentagon end its formal ban on women in combat roles.

Eric Fanning helped break a glass ceiling for the LGBTQ+ community and the United States military is stronger because of his involvement.

Technical Sergeant Leonard P. Matlovich

Vietnam War Veteran and Recipient of the Purple Heart and the Bronze Star

"When I was in the military they gave me a medal for killing two men, and a discharge for loving one."

Leonard P. Matlovich was born in Savannah, Georgia, on July 6, 1943. At age nineteen, he followed in his father's footsteps and enlisted in the United States Air Force, where he served for twelve years. During his tenure, he taught race relations classes to combat racism in the Air Force, served three tours of duty in Vietnam, and was awarded both the Bronze Star and the Purple Heart.

In 1975, he purposely outed himself to the Air Force to create a test case for challenging the ban on gays and lesbians serving in the military. Despite being a well-loved and well-decorated officer who served his country for over a decade, he was discharged in 1975 because of his sexual orientation. Matlovich fought this in court for years, and became a national hero along the way, appearing on the cover of *Time* magazine and the front page of the *New York Times*. He also appeared on numerous talk shows and news programs before eventually settling with the Air Force out of court.

Because his fight against discrimination in the military made him a household name, equal rights groups asked Matlovich to help with other LGBTQ+ causes. When Anita Bryant ran a Florida campaign to repeal a local ordinance prohibiting discrimination on the basis of sexual orientation, Matlovich helped campaigns fight against her. He also stepped up to battle the Briggs initiative, which tried to ban gay and lesbian people from teaching in California public schools. And when California tried to pass Proposition 64 (a bill that would have required people with HIV/AIDS to be isolated and quarantined), Matlovich protested against that, too.

Because of his dedicated service in the military, his fight for LGBTQ+ equality, and his mission to help people living

with HIV and AIDS, Leonard P. Matlovich is still a hero to
many people today. His tombstone, which is located in the
Congressional Cemetery in Washington, does not have his
name inscribed on it because he wanted it to be a memorial
for all gay veterans. Instead, it bears the quote, "When I was
in the military they gave me a medal for killing two men, and
a discharge for loving one." Many LGBTQ+ veterans have
chosen to be buried near him, and his gravesite became a
symbol of hope during the fight to repeal Don't Ask, Don't Tell.
It continues to be a symbol of hope today.

Part 6

MUSIC

Brandi Carlile

Grammy Award-Winning Singer, Songwriter, Musician, and Producer

"You don't have to be famous to be a hero, anyone can do that. I'll never be my heroes, but I'll always have 'em."

Brandi Carlile was born on June 1, 1981, in the rural town of Ravensdale, Washington, about thirty miles southeast of Seattle. Her mother was a local country singer and fostered a love for music in her daughter from a young age. When Carlile was eight years old, she performed Johnny Cash's hit, "Tennessee Flat-Top Box," alongside her mother, igniting her passion for singing live. She later learned how to play the piano and guitar, and started performing country songs with her mother and brother in a band called the Carliles; and yet, no one could have predicted that girl from a small town who lived in and out of poverty would go on to win eleven Grammy Awards and become a worldwide, musical sensation.

In 1999, Carlile met twin brother musicians, Phil and Tom Hanseroth, and she started performing with them in various Seattle clubs. Together, they recorded Carlile's self-titled debut album, *Brandi Carlile*, in 2005 and re-released it in 2006 with additional songs. The album was met with critical acclaim and *Rolling Stone* magazine named her one of the "10 Artists to Watch in 2005." Carlile continued to build on her success with subsequent releases, including *The Story* (2007), *Give Up the Ghost* (2009), *Bear Creek* (2012), and more, but it was *The Firewatcher's Daughter* (2015) that resulted in her first Grammy Nomination. As of 2024, she has racked up a total of twenty-six Grammy nominations and eleven wins. Carlile soon saw herself performing with some of the legends she looked up to as a kid, including people like Joni Mitchell, Dolly Parton, and Sir Elton John.

During the pandemic, Brandi Carlile wrote *Broken Horses: A Memoir* (2021) and received rave reviews from *The New York Times*, *Associated Press*, *Vulture*, and more. The book shot up to number 1 on *The New York Times* Best Sellers list, proving even outside of music, Carlile was an eloquent wordsmith.

In addition to being a singer, songwriter, performer, producer, and author, Carlile is also a tireless advocate for social and political causes. Along with her wife, Catherine Shepherd, and her bandmates, Tim and Phil Hanseroth, Brandi Carlile founded the Looking Out Foundation, a 501(c)3 charity focusing on the arts, women, health, education and environment, community development, and human and civil rights. The foundation has given away nearly $6 million to social justice and humanitarian causes locally in the US and around the world since its inception. Not only is Brandi Carlile one of the greatest musicians of our time, but she also uses her platform to create positive change in the world.

Sir Elton John

Grammy Award-Winning Singer, Songwriter, and Composer

"Better to build a bridge than a wall."

When it comes to music, Sir Elton John (born Reginald Kenneth Dwight on March 25, 1947) is one of the most iconic people in the industry. He's a singer, songwriter, and composer who taught himself how to play the piano when he was only four years old.

John took the music industry by storm, and with the help of various lyricists, such as Bernie Taupin, Tim Rice, and Gary Osborne, he spewed out a string of hits, making him one of the most popular musicians of the twentieth century. He dominated the singles charts, and even branched out into movie soundtracks and musicals. His song "Can You Feel the Love Tonight" (written for Disney's animated movie, *The Lion King*) won Best Original Song for both the Academy Awards and the Golden Globe Awards. He later teamed up with Lee Hall to adapt the movie *Billy Elliott* into a musical, and that show went on to win ten Tony Awards. John has had top 10 singles in the UK charts across six decades and he is one of the few artists who have earned an EGOT (Emmy, Grammy, Oscar, and Tony Awards).

In 1997, John released a rewritten version of his song "Candle in the Wind" as a tribute to his friend Diana, Princess of Wales, who had died in a horrific car accident. The single sold thirty-three million copies worldwide, and the proceeds went to Diana's charities. The Guinness World Records website lists it as the best-selling single since the US and UK singles charts began in the 1950s.

In addition to his musical success, John also contributes to various causes. Most notably, he created the Elton John AIDS Foundation to help raise money for education programs, direct care, and support services to those living with, or at high risk of contracting, HIV.

Other highlights of Elton John's career include receiving the Grammy Legend Award, induction into the Rock and Roll Hall of Fame, and ranking as the most successful male solo artist on the Billboard Hot 100 "Top 10 Artists of All Time" list in 2013. With all his success and contributions to the world, it's no wonder Queen Elizabeth dubbed him a knight.

John married his longtime partner, David Furnish, when same-sex marriage became legal in the UK. They have two children together.

k.d. lang

Grammy Award-Winning
Singer and Songwriter

"Look. Art knows no prejudice, art knows no boundaries, art doesn't really have judgment in its purest form. So just go, just go."

Nashville loved k.d. lang's voice, but didn't really know what to make of her. Born in 1961 in Alberta, Canada, she marched to her own drum and did things the way she wanted to. Some of her choices paid off, while some angered fans and caused boycotts. Still, lang rose to fame with her talent while never compromising her values.

In 1985, she won her first JUNO Award for Most Promising Female Vocalist, leading her to sign with an American record producer in Nashville, Tennessee, and release the critically acclaimed album, *Angel with a Lariat*. 1988 seemed to be her year, winning a Grammy Award for Best Country Collaboration with Vocals for "Crying" (a duet she did with Roy Orbison), being selected as the "Woman of the Year" by Canadian women's magazine *Chatelaine*, and garnering international recognition for her performance at the closing ceremony of the Calgary Winter Olympics.

With her androgynous style, lang continued her rise to fame, winning the Entertainer of the Year award from the Canadian Country Music Association three years in a row (1987-1989) and Female Artist of the Year in 1988 and 1989. There seemed to be no stopping her… until she joined a "Meat Stinks" campaign for PETA. "We all love animals," lang said in the ad, "but why do we call some of them pets and some of them dinner? If you knew how meat was made, you'd probably lose your lunch. I know, I'm from cattle country. That's why I became a vegetarian."

The backlash from "cattle country" was immediate and harsh. A sign identifying Consort, Alberta as the "Home of k.d. lang" was burned down, and various radio stations in Canada and the United States started pulling her music from the air. The boycott didn't hinder lang for long. In 1992, she came out as a lesbian in the June edition of the *Advocate*, and crossed music genres with the release of her album Ingénue. Her single "Constant Craving" became the biggest hit of her career, earning her another Grammy for Best Female Pop Vocal Performance.

Even though lang had experienced backlash for being an animal rights activist, that didn't stop her from continuing to speak out on issues she felt were important. She has since become an activist for LGBTQ+ equality, HIV/AIDS, and Tibetan human rights.

Her career continued to thrive, landing on VH-1's list of the 100 Greatest Women in Rock & Roll and CMT's list of the 40 Greatest Women in Country Music. She has a star on Canada's Walk of Fame, and in 2013, she was inducted into the Canadian Music Hall of Fame. Known for being true to herself and always standing up for what she believes in, k.d. lang has become a legend.

Leonard Bernstein

Tony and Grammy Award–
Winning Composer

*"This will be our reply to violence:
to make music more intensely, more beautifully,
more devotedly than ever before."*

Probably the greatest American composer, Leonard Bernstein defied classical music convention. He was classically trained at Harvard University and the Curtis Institute of Music, yet he wrote compositions for Broadway. He popularized Mahler's symphonies in the US, yet he peppered his pioneering television series, *Young People's Concerts with the New York Philharmonic,* with music from the Kinks.

Bernstein will probably be best remembered for his musical composition of the Tony Award-winning show *West Side Story*, a musical whose film adaptation won numerous Academy Awards. The modern beats he crafted, combined with bold and provocative social commentary, signaled a new beginning in musical theater. But Bernstein was so much more than a Broadway musical composer, having composed a violin concerto, three symphonies, and two operas. He also collaborated with Jerome Robbins to compose ballets and wrote the score for the award-winning film *On the Waterfront.*

As Bernstein was becoming better known around the world, rumors about his sexuality began to spread. Fearing that his career would suffer as a result, his mentor Mitropoulos suggested he get married. Even though Bernstein did get married and had three children with Chilean actress, Felicia Montealegre, it was no secret that he loved men. His wife even wrote in a letter, "You are a homosexual...our marriage is not based on passion but on tenderness and mutual respect."

Bernstein had a long-lasting friendship with the Kennedys. He was invited to participate in JFK's preinaugural gala, and conducted the National Symphony Orchestra in a piece he composed specifically for the event. He even participated in fundraisers with the Kennedys, including one event that helped raise money for the building now known as the John F. Kennedy Center for the Performing Arts. After JFK's assassination, Bernstein conducted Mahler's Symphony No. 2, Resurrection, in a televised memorial for the president. He performed again at Robert Kennedy's funeral in 1968.

During his career, Bernstein won sixteen Grammy Awards and multiple Tony Awards, and became a member of the American Theater Hall of Fame, but in addition to his musical contributions, Bernstein was also dedicated to making the world a better place. He won many prizes throughout his life and donated much of any prize money to humanitarian causes ranging from AIDS awareness and research to world peace. In 1989, he famously conducted the Berlin Celebration Concerts on both sides of the Berlin Wall as it was being dismantled.

Bernstein's impact was recognized around the world, and he has numerous decorations from the governments of Austria, Chile, Finland, France, West Germany, Italy, Israel, and Mexico. He truly is one of the greats.

Ricky Martin

Actor and Grammy Award-Winning Singer

*"If we, who are all here together on this earth,
don't take care of one another, then who else
will? It is our duty."*

From his early days singing in the teen group Menudo to becoming a Grammy Award-winning international pop star, Ricky Martin is hands-down one of the biggest Latin music stars in the world. He's known for his good looks, charming personality, generous heart, sexy dance moves, and of course, a distinctive, energetic voice that got the whole world to shake their *bon-bons*.

Born Enrique Jose Martin Morales IV, Ricky Martin sang for five years with the teen group Menudo before aging out at eighteen. He then focused on his solo acting and singing career. He had a recurring role on ABC's daytime soap opera, *General Hospital*, and he starred in the Broadway stage production of Les Misérables.

Martin was already well-known throughout the Latin and Hispanic communities from his early Menudo days and a few solo music albums in Spanish, but when he performed "La Copa de la Vida" ("The Cup of Life") at the 1998 World Cup soccer tournament in France, he suddenly became an international sensation. That performance was broadcast to two billion people around the world and became an instant hit. He performed the song again at the 1999 Grammy Awards, where he picked up an award for Best Latin Pop Performance. Martin continued to release hits, including the English single, "Livin' La Vida Loca," and his debut English album *Ricky Martin* (which debuted at number one on the Billboard chart), and because of his long-lasting success, Martin received a star on the Hollywood Walk of Fame on October 16, 2007.

In his spare time, Martin uses his fame to help those in need. He became a UNICEF Goodwill Ambassador and has worked to improve the rights of children worldwide. He also founded the Ricky Martin Foundation, which helps defend youth and fight against child exploitation and human trafficking. His philanthropic efforts don't stop there, though. He also helped with 2005 tsunami relief efforts in Thailand and with the 2017 hurricane relief efforts in Puerto Rico.

Martin also has a long history of helping in the fight against HIV/AIDS. He was a spokesperson for MAC's Viva Glam campaign (supporting organizations that provide services to people living with HIV/AIDS) and in 2016, he even auctioned off a passionate kiss at an amfAR charity event in Brazil. Guess how much that kiss went for: a whopping ninety thousand dollars!

In 2010, Ricky Martin came out of the closet by publishing an announcement on his website. "I am proud to say that I am a fortunate homosexual man. I am very blessed to be who I am."

Rob Halford

Lead Vocalist for the Grammy Award-Winning Heavy Metal Band, Judas Priest

"I think the last thing you want in life is to live with regret."

In 1998, Rob Halford shocked the world by coming out as a gay man during an interview with MTV. Sure, there had been other people in the music industry who were open about their sexuality at the time, but Halford was a heavy metal singer, and the genre was known for its aggression and hypermasculinity. Many people believed that a person could not be both gay and masculine, but Halford helped chip away at that stereotype.

Halford was born on August 25, 1951, in Sutton Coldfield, a town in England. In the early 1970s, he joined Judas Priest as lead singer, and the band went on to become one of the most influential metal bands in the world. The use of twin guitar harmonies, fast double bass drums, and high-pitched vocals distinguished the band from its contemporaries, and the versatility of Halford's voice, going from a deep throaty growl to an operatic, screaming falsetto, made their music instantly recognizable.

In addition to their music, Judas Priest also became trendsetters in fashion. They had an extreme biker look onstage as early as 1978, wearing leather and studs from head to toe. Their look influenced the style of other bands such as Metallica, Slipknot, and more.

Halford left Judas Priest in 1992 to pursue other projects. During his time away, he was the lead singer of Fight, 2wo (sometimes referred to as Two), and Halford before returning as lead singer of Judas Priest in 2003. His coming out as a gay man did not hinder the band in any way; in fact, they went on to win a Grammy in 2009 for Best Metal Performance with their album *Dissident Aggressor*.

As frontman for Judas Priest and one of the first openly gay metal stars, Rob Halford is a true pioneer in the music industry.

Part 7

RELIGION

Camille Shira Angel

First Rabbi-in-Residence at the University of San Francisco

"I will be coming out in public conversations until the day when we see full acceptance and inclusion, mental well-being, and thriving LGBTQIA+ young people."

Rabbi Camille Shira Angel, born in Southern California in 1965, is a ninth-generation rabbi and graduate of the Hebrew Union College Jewish Institute of Religion in New York City. She says, "I grew up surrounded by lots of rabbis, whether as friends or family. My sister even married a rabbi. It was sort of like the family business." When Sally Priesand became the first American female rabbi in 1972, Rabbi Angel was inspired knowing that her gender would not be a barrier to her calling. But later, when she realized she was a lesbian, she worried about whether or not she'd be allowed to enter seminary. That worry subsided when her Reform seminary made the decision to ordain lesbians and gays as rabbis in 1990.

Rabbi Angel's twenty-nine years of service started in 1995 at *Congregation Rodeph Sholom* on the Upper West Side, where she helped transform a mainstream congregation into a more inclusive community that opened its doors to a number of people in the LGBTQ+ community. She then went on to serve as the senior rabbi of the Reform LGBTQ+ *Congregation Sha'ar Zahav* in San Francisco, where she edited and contributed to an inclusive, LGBTQ+ prayer book, *Siddur Sha'ar Zahav* (2009). During her time there from 2000–2015, she administered to her flock for all their high and low points, from births to weddings, from illnesses to memorials. She was chosen for her "rabbinical countenance and ability to listen," according to David Gellman, then president of Sha'ar Zahav.

Rabbi Angel has been recognized for her significant contributions over the years. She was honored as a member of Letty Cottin Pogrobin's "List of Top 50 Rabbis" and recipient of the Emanuel Gamoran Curriculum Award. In 2010, she was invited to the White House by President Barack and Michelle Obama to celebrate Chanukah, and in 2022, the Hebrew Union

College Jewish Institute of Religion in Los Angeles recognized Rabbi Angel's body of work by awarding her an honorary doctorate in divinity.

Rabbi Angel lives in San Francisco with her wife. In 2019, the University of San Francisco (USF) appointed her as a rabbi-in-residence, marking the first time a rabbi was appointed by the Jesuit Catholic university in its 169-year history. Her daughter is a proud graduate of USF. Rabbi Angel is both a spiritual advisor to students and an adjunct professor in the Swig Program of Jewish Studies and Social Justice, one of the first in the world. Of her work, Rabbi Angel says, "Having the opportunity to share the genius of Judaism, the creativity, the commitment to *tikkun olam* (repairing the world) and the way we do that as Jews, to a student body that isn't familiar with them, it's renewed my deep love of my spiritual inheritance."

Archbishop Carl Bean

Religious Leader

"My life is testimony to one statement and one statement only: God is love, and love is for everybody."

Archbishop Carl Bean was born into a life of poverty but after years of adversity, he would go on to become a leader in the community, spreading hope and light to those around him. He released the surprise Motown hit, "I Was Born This Way," in the 1970s, and the unique song featured Bean belting out his pride in being gay. That was something the music industry hadn't really heard before, and the gay disco anthem spread through the clubs like wildfire. The song catapulted him to fame and led him to work with musical legends such as Dionne Warwick, Burt Bacharach, Miles Davis, and Sammy Davis Jr. But it was during the early 1980s that Bean found his true calling: serving others as an openly gay ordained minister during the height of the AIDS crisis.

Bean founded the Unity Fellowship of Christ Church, a church for openly gay and lesbian African-Americans. He also created the Minority AIDS Project through the church, the first community-based HIV/AIDS organization established and managed by people of color in the United States. The Project provided housing, transportation, outreach, HIV prevention, HIV testing, case management, and mental health services.

"In the gay community, they said Silence = Death," Bean told *POZ* magazine. "That personally spoke to me, that you can't be silent now, you can't let people die around you. I just knew I had love for my fellow human beings and that the Christ consciousness in me said, 'I am my brother's keeper.'"

The church continues to spread Bean's message that "God Is Love and Love Is For Everyone." As for his music, "I Was Born This Way" made a comeback after being remixed in the 1980s, and the song has been remixed multiple times since then. Bean's message of love and self-acceptance continues to resonate with people across the country.

Bishop Gene Robinson

First Openly Gay Bishop Elected to the Episcopal Church

"It seems to me that if God calls us to anything it's to a life of integrity."

Twelve years before the Supreme Court legalized same-sex marriage in the United States, something significant happened. At the time, there were no federal hate crime protections for LGBTQ+ people, and "Don't Ask, Don't Tell" was in full effect, banning gays and lesbians from openly serving in the military. Thirteen states still had sodomy laws in place, giving them a legal way to persecute people in the community. Even with all the animosity against those who identified as LGBTQ+, Gene Robinson was elected bishop by the New Hampshire diocese in 2003, paving the way for him to become the first openly gay person to be a consecrated bishop in the Episcopal Church.

His elevation to bishop upset many and created a schism in the church, resulting in approximately one hundred thousand people leaving for the more conservative Anglican Church in North America. Regardless, Robinson risked everything, including his safety, for what he believed he was called to do. In November of 2003, he was officially consecrated in front of an audience of four thousand, including his parents, former wife, children, and partner. During the ceremony, Robinson was surrounded by bodyguards, and even had to wear a bulletproof vest under his robes because of the death threats he was getting. Those death threats continued for years and ultimately played a big role in his decision to retire in 2013. Before retiring, though, he led a very public life doing good in the name of the church.

During his time as a church leader, Robinson was an AIDS educator in both the US and Africa. He also spent a lot of time ministering to those in prison and was an advocate for many causes, including racial equality, debt relief for impoverished nations, socially responsible investment, and access to health care for the uninsured. In addition, Robinson lobbied for full civil marriage rights and equal protection under the law for all LGBTQ+ people. He even advised Barack Obama on LGBTQ+ equality issues during his first presidential campaign and delivered the invocation at President Obama's inauguration.

Robinson has inspired people around the world to hope. His story was featured in the documentary *For the Bible Tells Me So*, which won numerous awards, including Best Documentary at the Seattle International Film Festival and the Grand Jury Prize at the 2007 Sundance Film Festival. He has done much more than lead the Episcopal Church. Robinson has helped many people feel welcomed in a place where they previously felt ostracized. He helped make the Episcopal Church a beacon of inclusion.

Part 8

SCIENCE, HEALTH, AND TECHNOLOGY

Lynn Conway

Computer Scientist and Electrical Engineer

"People tend to be blind to innovations made by 'others,' or those they don't expect to make innovations. People usually don't notice when something that has never been done before is happening right in front of their eyes."

D o you have a cell phone? Have you ever played a video game? Do you use a PC to do your work? Chances are that you answered *"yes"* to all of these questions, but did you know that each of these devices as we know them wouldn't have been possible without the innovation and creativity of a transgender woman?

American computer scientist and electrical engineer Lynn Conway was born on January 2, 1938, in Mount Vernon, NY. She was an inquisitive kid who loved math and science, and even built a reflecting telescope with a six-inch mirror when she was only sixteen years old. She went on to study physics at MIT and ultimately earned her bachelor's and master's degrees in electrical engineering at Columbia University.

Conway took on a position at IBM where she worked on designing the world's fastest supercomputer, but when she came out to the company in 1968 and informed them of her decision to transition, IBM fired her. Most of her friends, family members, and colleagues cut her off as well and it was difficult for her to find work post-transition. It was a challenging and dark time for Conway, but she eventually persevered in finding contract work and ultimately landed a job at Xerox, where she changed the world as we knew it.

While at Xerox in the 1970s, Conway worked with Carver Mead of the California Institute of Technology and the two of them developed a process called Very Large Scale Integration (VLSI), a groundbreaking method of microchip design that allowed millions of individual components to be integrated onto one microchip. Conway and Mead co-authored a textbook, *Introduction to VLSI Systems*, which became a standard handbook for computer science and engineering students.

The VLSI design technique quickly spread around the world and fueled the development of cheaper and more powerful microprocessors. It revolutionized the tech industry, becoming fundamental to the fabrication of modern CPUs (Central Processing Units) used in computers, smartphones, and tablets. VLSI also allowed for devices to become smaller and more portable while at the same time increasing their performance, reliability, and functionality, leading to a wide range of modern technologies including but not limited to digital cameras, gaming consoles, home appliances, routers, and smart TVs. We even use it in automotive applications like navigation systems, infotainment systems, and advanced driver assistance systems (ADAS).

Conway went on to win numerous awards, including the 2009 Computer Pioneer Award from the Institute of Electrical and Electronics Engineers and the 2015 James Clerk Maxwell Medal from the IEEE and the Royal Society of Edinburgh. She was also recognized by *Time* magazine as one of "21 Transgender People Who Influenced American Culture." But even with all her success, IBM remained silent. It wasn't until 2020 that IBM formally apologized for firing her fifty-two years earlier. The company invited Conway to a virtual event where they formally apologized and presented her with the IBM Lifetime Achievement Award for her achievements both during her time at IBM and throughout her career.

Lynn Conway died on June 9, 2024, but her legacy continues to inspire countless individuals in the fields of computer science and engineering. Through her pioneering work and her fearless advocacy for LGBTQ+ equality, Lynn has left an unforgettable mark on the world of technology and beyond.

Admiral Rachel L. Levine, MD

Assistant Secretary for Health in the US Department of Health and Human Services

"The pandemic has taught us like nothing before how interconnected we all are."

As the highest-ranking openly transgender government official in US history, Admiral Rachel L. Levine, MD is a rock star. She began her medical journey after graduating from Harvard College and Tulane University School of Medicine. She then completed her training in Pediatrics and Adolescent Medicine at the Mt. Sinai Medical Center in New York City.

In 2015, ADM Levine became Pennsylvania's Physician General after being unanimously confirmed by Pennsylvania's state senate, and in 2018, she was named Pennsylvania's Secretary of Health. During her tenure in state government, ADM Levine focused on various public health issues, including the opioid crisis, maternal health, childhood vaccinations, eating disorders, and the implementation of medical marijuana programs.

In 2021, ADM Levine was thrust into the national spotlight when President Joe Biden nominated her to serve as the Assistant Secretary for Health for the US Department of Health and Human Services (HHS). After being confirmed by the US Senate in a bipartisan vote, she became the first openly transgender person to hold a Senate-confirmed position at the federal level and the highest-ranking openly transgender government official in US history.

In her new role, one of the main things Dr. Levine was responsible for was helping to coordinate the government's response to the COVID-19 pandemic. This included things like developing public health guidance related to COVID-19, participating in public communications efforts to educate people on the risks and prevention measures of the virus, overseeing the distribution of vaccines, and much more. Under her leadership, Dr. Levine also oversaw the formation of the

Office of Long COVID Research and Practice which was responsible for coordinating the federal government's ongoing response to the longer-term effects of COVID-19.

In October 2021, Levine was sworn in as a four-star admiral in the US Public Health Service Commissioned Corps (USPHS), becoming the first openly transgender four-star officer in the nation's eight uniformed services and the first female four-star admiral of the USPHS. Considering all of these accomplishments, it's no wonder she was named one of *USA Today's* Women of the Year in 2022. Throughout her career, ADM Levine has been a trailblazer and advocate for public health, LGBTQ+ rights, and healthcare equity. Her leadership has not only advanced medical practices and policies but also inspired countless individuals around the world.

Alan Turing

War Hero and Father of Computer Science

"Sometimes it is the people who no one imagines anything of who do the things that no one can imagine."

It was the height of World War II, the deadliest war in history, resulting in more than fifty million deaths. The Germans were using the Enigma machine as their primary way of ciphering messages and war commands. Their superior encryption technology was giving them an upper hand in the war until Alan Turing, a gay man, cracked the code and helped turn the tide of the war.

Turing, born on June 23, 1912 in London, England, was one of the greatest mathematical minds of the twentieth century. He attended the University of Cambridge and received a PhD from Princeton University. He then took a job at the Government Code and Cypher School (GCCS), where he led a team of code breakers instrumental in ending WWII.

During the war, German U-boats were intercepting cargoes of essential supplies for Great Britain. Turing broke the Enigma code they were using to exchange critical information, enabling Britain to determine the location of the U-boats and thus avoid or destroy them. Turing and his team helped decode numerous other intercepted messages, too, giving the Allies the upper hand in the war. Some military historians believe that Turing helped shorten the war by two or more years, and that, without his efforts, an estimated two million more lives would have been lost. Because of his significant code-breaking work, he was made an Officer of the Most Excellent Order of the British Empire.

All of this is impressive on its own, but Alan Turing was more than just a code-breaker. He also came up with a hypothetical machine capable of computing anything that is computable, basically an early concept of a programmable digital computer.

So basically, if you've ever typed on a computer or smartphone, you can thank Turing for making that possible.

Sadly, though, Turing was a victim of his time. In 1952, he called the police to report a break-in, but when they found out he had a sexual relationship with the perpetrator, Turing was charged with "gross indecency" for being gay and was given the choice of either going to prison or undergoing chemical castration. He chose the latter. Because of his conviction, Turing also lost his security clearance and, as a result, was no longer allowed to work at the GCCS. What a great way to treat a war hero, right?

Almost sixty years after his death, Turing was posthumously granted a royal pardon by Queen Elizabeth II. Not long after that, the British government passed Turing's Law, posthumously pardoning gay and bisexual men who had been convicted for homosexual acts in the past. We've come a long way since the British government punished Turing for being gay. If he were alive today, how do you think he would feel knowing that the world's largest technology company, Apple, is run by Tim Cook, an openly gay man?

Sally Ride, PhD

First American Woman in Space

"You can't be what you can't see."

All of NASA's astronauts used to be men. That was until Dr. Sally Ride and five other women were chosen to join NASA's astronaut class in 1978. Dr. Ride eventually became the first American woman to go into space when she flew on the space shuttle Challenger on June 18, 1983.

It took a while for NASA to adapt to having female astronauts. In addition to suggesting women take one hundred tampons with them for a one-week flight in space, NASA engineers also assumed women would want to bring special makeup kits on the journey, and asked Dr. Ride to help them develop one. The press didn't know what to think about women going into space, either. They wanted to know if the flight would affect Dr. Ride's reproductive organs and whether she cried when they had malfunctions in the simulator. Even though Dr. Ride had a doctorate in physics and was clearly capable of doing the same work as her male co-workers, many people focused on her gender rather than her qualifications.

Despite the misconceptions people had regarding female astronauts, Dr. Ride proved that she was more than capable of doing her job. She served in space on two flights, was appointed to help investigate space shuttle disasters, and even led the task force responsible for NASA's long-range and strategic planning.

Dr. Ride retired from NASA in 1987 and went on to teach at Stanford, and later at the University of California, San Diego. In 2001, she founded Sally Ride Science with her partner, Tam O'Shaughnessy, and a small group of their colleagues. The company was created to motivate girls and young women to pursue careers in science, technology, engineering, and math.

Dr. Ride died of pancreatic cancer in 2012, and just before she passed away, she left the decision to make her sexual orientation public to O'Shaughnessy, her partner of twenty-seven years. Dr. Ride's obituary listed O'Shaughnessy as her surviving partner.

Even after her death, Dr. Ride's legacy continues to inspire people. President Barack Obama posthumously awarded her the Presidential Medal of Freedom (the nation's highest civilian honor), and the US Navy named a research vessel after her. Ray Mabus, Secretary of the Navy, said he named the ship after Dr. Ride to "encourage generations of students to continue exploring, discovering, and reaching for the stars." The US Postal Service also created a stamp with Dr. Ride's image on it, saying that she "inspired the nation as a pioneering astronaut, brilliant physicist, and dedicated educator." Dr. Sally Ride isn't just a role model to the LGBTQ+ community; she's one of America's greatest heroes.

Part 9

SPORTS

Megan Rapinoe

NWSL Player, Forward

FIFA Women's World Cup Champion and Olympic Gold Medalist

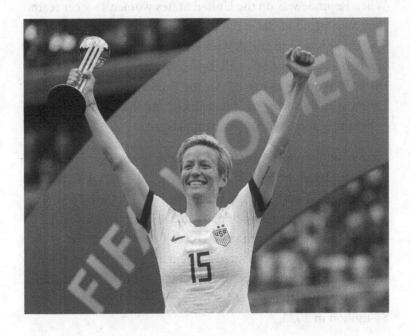

"Some people play best when they're frustrated and mad. I play my best when I'm happy. I really, truly do."

Megan Rapinoe was born a twin on July 5, 1985, and grew up in a large family in Redding, California. At five years old, she wanted to join a soccer team, but couldn't find a girls' team where she lived, so she joined the boys' team instead. She excelled at the game. After finishing high school, she attended the University of Portland on a soccer scholarship and won the 2005 national championship. She went on to become an Olympic gold medalist and one of the most influential figures in modern soccer.

When Rapinoe was on the United States women's soccer team, they won a gold medal at the 2012 London Summer Olympics. The US also won the FIFA Women's World Cup in 2015 and again in 2019. Rapinoe's stellar performance on the field in the 2019 World Cup earned her the Golden Boot for scoring the most goals during the tournament and the Golden Ball for being the best overall tournament player.

As one of the most recognized figures in women's soccer, Rapinoe played the bulk of her professional career with the Seattle Reign Football Club. From 2013–2023, she helped turn around a team struggling to make goals. Despite injuries and shortened seasons, Rapinoe was often the leading scorer. Her accomplishments contributed to securing major endorsements from Nike, Samsung, Procter & Gamble, Hulu, LUNA Bar, and Visa. According to *Forbes*, Megan Rapinoe's net worth grew to $7 million in 2023.

But Rapinoe's accomplishments extended beyond the field and she used her platform to address various social issues, including LGBTQ+ rights, gender equality, and racial justice. She publicly came out as gay in 2012, and throughout her career remained a vocal advocate for LGBTQ+ rights. Her activism gained widespread attention in 2016 when she took a knee during the national anthem in solidarity with NFL player Colin Kaepernick's protest against racial injustice.

Rapinoe was a leading voice in the fight for equal pay for female athletes. In 2016, she joined players Carli Lloyd, Hope Solo, Alex Morgan, and Becky Sauerbrunn to file an equal pay complaint with the Equal Employment Opportunity Commission against the US Soccer Federation. The complaint stated that according to the USSF's 2015 financial report, "despite the women's team generating nearly $20 million more revenue last year than the US men's team, the women are paid almost four times less." The complaint went nowhere, so Rapinoe and twenty-seven of her teammates filed a lawsuit against the US Soccer Federation. They settled with the women sharing $24 million and the federation agreeing to equalize pay.

In 2022, President Joe Biden awarded Megan Rapinoe the Presidential Medal of Freedom, the nation's highest civilian honor. A few months later, on January 5, 2023, Biden signed the Equal Pay for Team USA Act into law, ensuring equal pay and benefits for all athletes who represent the US in global athletic competitions, regardless of gender.

Megan Rapinoe's legacy is defined not just by her incredible skill and achievements in soccer but also by her courage to speak out and fight for social justice. With her fiancé, basketball legend Sue Bird, Rapinoe launched a production company, A Touch More, centering on stories of revolutionaries who move culture forward.

Billie Jean King

Tennis Champion and Pioneer
for Social Justice

"A champion is afraid of losing.
Everyone else is afraid of winning."

B illie Jean King had an epiphany when she was twelve years old, playing on the public tennis courts in Long Beach. Everybody wore white—white clothes, white shoes, white socks—and everyone who played was white as well. Seeing the lack of diversity in the sport, she became determined to fight for equal rights and opportunities for boys and girls. King made it her life commitment to ensure that people could play tennis no matter their country of origin, their gender, or their race. But the disparity in sports was great, and in order to have the ability to make a difference, King felt she had to be the best in her field. As time would tell, that's exactly what she became...the best.

King is now considered one of the greatest tennis players of all time. During her career, she had won a total of thirty-nine Grand Slam career titles. She was also the first female athlete to ever be named *Sports Illustrated* Sportsperson of the Year. In 1971, she hit a major milestone when she became the first female athlete to earn over one hundred thousand dollars in prize money in a single season of competition, but her paycheck was still smaller than the paychecks of her male peers. After winning the US Open in 1972, she threatened to boycott the event going forward if the women's prize money did not match the men's. The US Open gave in, and the following year it became the first major tournament to award equal prize money to men and women.

King became the first president of the Women's Tennis Association in 1973, and her stature as a leader in the feminist movement grew, so when Bobby Riggs (American tennis champion and self-proclaimed "male chauvinist") challenged King to a "Battle of the Sexes," the world paid attention. Riggs claimed that female games were inferior and that he could beat any of the top female players. King agreed to compete against him in a televised match referred to as the "Battle of the Sexes." An estimated ninety million people around the world watched King pulverize Riggs 6–4, 6–3, and 6–3. King made history, proving women were not inferior to men in sports, and in fact, can even be better. The defining moment was later retold in the 2017 movie *Battle of the Sexes*, starring Emma Stone and Steve Carell.

Shortly after the highly publicized match with Riggs, King went on to cofound World Team Tennis, a co-ed league where men and women play a five-set competition in a mix of singles, doubles, and mixed doubles. She also created the Women's Sports Foundation, an organization dedicated to advancing the lives of girls and women through sport and physical activity.

While still married to her husband, King was outed when a palimony lawsuit filed against her by female ex-partner, Marilyn Barnett, became public. She lost major endorsements and faced public backlash because of the affair. King remained married to her husband for a few more years, but they eventually divorced, after she fell in love with her doubles partner, Ilana Kloss. She now lives out and proud.

In 1987, King was inducted into the International Tennis Hall of Fame, and in 2009, she received the Presidential Medal of Freedom for her record of championing human rights, both on and off the court. While there's still a long way to go before we reach full equality, we wouldn't have come this far if it weren't for Billie Jean King.

Esera Tuaolo

NFL Player, Defensive Lineman

"Be welcoming to athletes based on their skills, not based on who they love."

E sera Tuaolo basically lived the American dream. He was born in Hawaii to a family of banana farmers, and grew up in poverty, living with eight brothers and sisters in a dirt-floored hut. He worked hard, graduated college, and went on to have a thriving career in football lasting thirteen years, nine of which were in the NFL.

Tuaolo's talent was recognized early on. He played college football at Oregon State University, and in 1989, he won the Morris Trophy for most outstanding defensive lineman in the league. The Green Bay Packers drafted him the following year, and his professional sports career took off. During his time with the NFL, he played for five teams: the Packers plus the Minnesota Vikings, Jacksonville Jaguars, Atlanta Falcons, and Carolina Panthers. He won the NFC Championship with the Atlanta Falcons and made it all the way to Super Bowl XXXIII, playing against the Denver Broncos.

Even though Tuaolo had a successful career, the stress of being gay and living in the closet took a toll on him. He eventually retired from the NFL, and in 2002, the six-foot-three, three-hundred-pound Samoan football player shattered stereotypes by publicly coming out of the closet on HBO's *Real Sports*. A few years later, he followed up with even more personal details about his life in his autobiography *Alone in the Trenches: My Life As a Gay Man in the NFL*.

Since coming out, Tuaolo has fought for LGBTQ+ equality and worked on anti-bullying campaigns. He became a board member for the Gay and Lesbian Athletics Foundation and an Advisory Board Member for the You Can Play Project, and he has also worked with the NFL to combat homophobia.

In 2017, Tuaolo stunned the nation once again when he competed on Season Thirteen of *The Voice*, showing everyone that he could sing! While he didn't win the competition, he was able to showcase his stunning vocals, and America welcomed him into their hearts.

Whatever Tuaolo does, it always seems to somehow tie back in to sports. His singing career has led him to perform the National Anthem at sporting events including NFL, MLB, NHL, and NBA games. When he isn't serenading people with his vocal cords, Tuaolo continues to use his voice to speak out for equality. In 2018, he hosted the first annual Inclusion Party at the Super Bowl, benefiting LGBTQ+ charities in Minneapolis. It was attended by NFL players and various other athletes.

As a gay man with the body of a football player and the voice of an angel, Tuaolo has shown the world that LGBTQ+ people don't all fit into one small box. We come in all shapes and sizes, and if we work hard and follow our dreams, we can do anything. We can make the world a more inclusive place, and we can even play in the Super Bowl.

Jason Collins

NBA Player, Center

"I think it's important for all of us to celebrate and support everyone to live an authentic life."

Jason Collins always loved basketball, and he was good at it, too. While in high school, he played in two state championships. In college, he played for the Stanford Cardinals, setting a school record for field goal percentage (.608) and ranking all-time third in blocks (89). His NBA career started when he played for the New Jersey Nets in 2001. He wound up making it to nine playoffs during his career, which lasted thirteen NBA seasons.

After the 2012–2013 season ended, Collins made national headlines when he came out as gay. "I'm a thirty-four-year-old NBA center. I'm black. And I'm gay," he wrote in the *Sports Illustrated* cover story. The online version drew 3.7 million unique visitors to the *Sports Illustrated* website. Collins became a free agent, but when he signed a contract with the Nets in 2014, he became the first openly gay active athlete to play in any of the four major US pro sports leagues. Collins chose to wear jersey number 98 in honor of Matthew Shepard, who was murdered in 1998 for being gay. His jersey immediately became the top-selling one at the NBA's online store, and the proceeds were donated to GLSEN and the Matthew Shepard Foundation. In 2014, *Time* magazine featured Collins on their cover and included him on their 100 Most Influential People in the World list.

After that season, Collins retired. He has since dedicated a significant amount of time to charity work, from helping fight childhood obesity to raising money for children of police officers killed on duty. In 2016, he traveled the country to help register people to vote in swing states, and even spoke at the Democratic National Convention.

Collins has secured his place in history and has inspired people around the country both on and off the court.

Stephen Alexander

America's First Openly Transgender Middle School & High School Coach

"Sports are about working with people for a common goal. It's about being part of something larger than yourself."

Stephen Alexander always excelled in sports. During his high school years, he played softball, tennis, basketball, volleyball, and soccer, and collectively, his teams won six state championships. He was well liked by his teammates, and over the course of his high school career, won multiple MVP awards. There was only one problem. All of these achievements were made while playing on girls' teams, and Alexander identified as male.

During college, Alexander came out to his family and began the journey of transitioning. Shortly thereafter, he moved to New York, where he spent time with writers, artists, and activists who also identified as trans/non-binary. After his sister had a baby, Stephen returned home to Rhode Island in order to be the uncle he dreamed he could be.

It wasn't long before Alexander heard about a middle school nearby that needed someone to coach its soccer team. He filled that role and soon found himself coaching the school's basketball, baseball, and tennis teams too. Coaching high school soccer, volleyball, and tennis soon followed.

In 2013, *OutSports* profiled Alexander, calling him "America's First Publicly Out Transgender High School Coach." The story went viral, and Alexander soon saw himself talked about in various news outlets. Nervous at first that there might be a backlash, he was pleasantly surprised when all the coverage seemed to be positive. He was even named one of *Sports Illustrated's* "Trailblazers of the Year" in 2014, and the high school he had attended inducted him into their Athletic Hall of Fame.

In response to all the love and support he received after coming out on the national stage, Alexander became a public speaker, helping schools and organizations better understand issues related to diversity in sports and education. He spends his time promoting inclusivity for all, and stands by his mantra: Everyone Can Play.

Part 10

LITERATURE

James Baldwin

Award-Winning Novelist, Essayist, and Playwright

"Not everything that is faced can be changed, but nothing can be changed until it is faced."

James Baldwin was born on August 2, 1924, in Harlem, a neighborhood in New York City. He grew up with a love for books, reading Charles Dickens, Harriet Beecher Stowe, and Fyodor Dostoevsky by fifth grade. This was seen as problematic in the eyes of his stepfather, a Baptist preacher who discouraged his reading, seeing it as the road to hell. Despite his stepfather's disdain for literature, James Baldwin went on to become one of the most prolific writers of the twentieth century.

Baldwin's teachers recognized his brilliant mind early on and recommended he visit the public library in Harlem, a place that became his sanctuary. One of his teachers, Orilla "Bill" Miller, took him to an all-Black rendition of Orson Welles' take on *Macbeth*, igniting Baldwin's desire to become a playwright. Miller later directed the first play that Baldwin ever wrote. Another one of his teachers, Harlem Renaissance poet Countee Cullen, ignited Baldwin's interest in Paris. Even though he was influenced by many teachers and advisors throughout his school years, Baldwin felt an obligation to help support his large family, so he quit high school in 1941 and took a series of menial jobs that later informed his essays about living as a Black man in America.

In 1948, with only forty dollars to his name, Baldwin moved to Paris, France, in the hopes that time away in a new setting would help him finish his first novel, *Go Tell It on the Mountain*. His move was successful. The book (which featured themes of race, religion, and sexuality) was published in 1953 to critical acclaim. It would go on to be included in the list of 100 Best English-Language Novels of the Twentieth Century by the Modern Library and the 100 Best English-Language Novels Released from 1923 to 2005 by *Time* magazine. Paris also served as the backdrop for his second novel, *Giovanni's*

Room, which was published in 1956. That book was more controversial at the time with its themes focusing on masculinity, sexuality, and class.

Living in Europe had a big impact on Baldwin because it took him out of the American bubble. He was able to escape from the racial and sexual discrimination he faced in the United States and he was able to explore his sexuality in a supportive environment. While Baldwin had relationships with both men and women, he resisted sexuality and gender-related labels because language changes over time. Instead, he favored being referred to as someone who chose love regardless of its recipient.

While abroad, he began to understand racism in a global context and it gave him a broader perspective on the American struggle for civil rights. This helped shape how he spoke about racial justice. In 1957, he returned to the US to participate in the Civil Rights Movement. He became a pivotal figure, using his writing and speaking to influence public opinion and advance the cause of racial justice. Baldwin often highlighted the intersectionality of race, class, gender, and other social issues, urging a broader, more inclusive approach to civil rights. This resonated with many civil rights activists and leaders, and Baldwin soon found himself connecting with people like Martin Luther King Jr. and Malcom X. These relationships were detailed in his unfinished manuscript, *Remember This House*, the basis for Raoul Peck's 2016 award-winning documentary, *I Am Not Your Negro*.

James Baldwin died from stomach cancer in 1987, but his impact is still felt today. In 2019, Regina King won an Oscar for Best Supporting Actress for *If Beale Street Could Talk* based on Baldwin's novel of the same name. Even President Barack Obama was inspired by Baldwin, growing up reading his books and channeling Baldwin when writing his own memoir, *A Promised Land*. In a 2020 interview with the *New York Times*, Obama said, "When I think about how I learned to write, who I mimicked, the voice that always comes to mind the most is James Baldwin." When it comes to authors who have made the biggest impact on society, James Baldwin is one of the greatest.

Mary Oliver

Pulitzer Prize and National Book Award-Winning Poet

"I've always wanted to write poems and nothing else."

Mary Oliver was born in Maple Heights, Ohio, in 1935 and spent much of her childhood outside, enjoying long walks in nature. She developed an early love of reading, and by the time she was twenty-eight years old had published her first book of poetry, *No Voyage and Other Poems,* in 1963. Now, with well over thirty books in print and a career spanning over half a century, Oliver is widely acknowledged as one of America's most beloved and best-selling poets.

When her sixth book of poetry, *American Primitive,* won the Pulitzer Prize in 1984, everyone asked, "Who's Mary Oliver?" Until then, she had not given even one reading and was leading a quiet life in Provincetown.

Later, she won the prestigious National Book Award for her collection, *New & Selected Poems,* in 1992. Oliver's unique ability to capture the essence of life through poems about animals, plants, the sky, and nature has inspired millions around the world, including Maria Shriver, American journalist and former First Lady of California. Shriver, who interviewed Oliver for *O, The Oprah Magazine* after six years of trying to secure an interview, connected with Oliver's uplifting poetry whose themes of love, survival, gratitude, and joy touch everyone.

One of Oliver's most well-known poems is "The Summer Day," which is often referred to as "The Grasshopper." It ends with the famous and frequently quoted line, "What is it you plan to do with your one wild and precious life?" That one line has radically changed the course of many people's lives, inviting them to look at the bigger picture and decide what's most important to them. Another of Oliver's popular poems is "Wild Geese," which reminds readers that you don't have to be perfect to be alive, you just have to let the animal in you love what it loves.

Even later in her career, Oliver has continued to captivate audiences. At the 2010 California Women's Conference, she shared the stage with other prominent women, including former First Ladies Laura Bush and Michelle Obama, and Supreme Court Justices Ruth Bader Ginsburg and Sandra Day O'Connor. In 2012, readers honored her with the Goodreads Choice Award for Best Poetry.

Many of Oliver's books are dedicated to her partner, photographer and bookstore owner Molly Malone Cook, who died in 2005. Oliver called their relationship a forty-year conversation between artists. In 2019, Oliver died from lymphoma at the age of 83. Though she grew up in a "very dark and broken house," she rose above that, saying, "What I have done is learn to love and learn to be loved and that didn't come easy."

Oscar Wilde

Poet, Novelist, and Playwright

*"To live is the rarest thing in the world.
Most people exist, that is all."*

Oscar Wilde always dazzled with his words. Born in Dublin in 1854 to a surgeon father and a poet mother, he became one of London's most famous playwrights. More than a hundred years after his death, his plays are among the most widely performed in the English language, and his wit and political satire are just as meaningful today as when they were written.

Best known for his thinly veiled gay novel, *The Picture of Dorian Gray* (1890), universally panned at the time of publication, his first and only novel nonetheless put Wilde at the center of controversy and curiosity. His next years were prolific, bringing *Lady Windemere's Fan* (1892), *A Woman of No Importance* (1893), *An Ideal Husband* (1895) and *The Importance of Being Earnest* (1895), to the forefront of the London stage.

His writings exposed Victorian hypocrisy including social and gender double standards. His work continues to be adapted for stage and film, garnering awards including Golden Globe and Academy Awards. Films and plays based on Wilde or his work have attracted top-tier talent, including Liam Neeson, Julianne Moore, Angela Lansbury, Judi Dench, Stephen Fry, Jude Law, Cate Blanchett, Helen Hunt, Minnie Driver, and others. In 2018, Wilde's short story *The Happy Prince* was made into a film starring Rupert Everett, Colin Firth, Emily Watson. and Tom Wilkinson.

In 1884, Wilde married Constance Lloyd, a wealthy Englishwoman. The couple had two sons, Cyril and Vyvyan, whom Wilde adored. However, in 1893, Wilde became infatuated with Lord Alfred Douglas and the two began a tempestuous affair. When Douglas' father, the Marquess of Queensberry, found out about the affair, he accused Wilde of sodomy, an illegal act at the time. Wilde sued Queensberry for libel, but dropped the lawsuit after it became clear that his private encounters with men would be exposed. But it was too late. The court came to the conclusion that Wilde had broken the law. He was later arrested and charged with "gross indecency." Wilde was convicted and sentenced to two years of hard labor from which, many say, he never recovered. Upon release, he moved to Paris under an assumed name and died in 1900 of meningitis at the age of forty-six. He is buried alongside celebrities in the Père Lachaise Cemetery.

Wilde was a victim of his time, persecuted during his life, but celebrated after his death. Now, many students study Wilde alongside other literary greats such as Charles Dickens, Jane Austen, and Shakespeare. His legacy lives on, inspiring millions of people to be their best selves and not take life too seriously.

Tony Kushner

Award-Winning Playwright and Screenwriter

*"The only thing an artist has to do
is to try and tell the truth."*

Tony Kushner was born in New York City in 1956 to musician parents, but the family moved to Lake Charles, Louisiana, shortly after his birth. His childhood experience of growing up Jewish in the deeply Christian South, in addition to suppressing any conscious awareness of his sexual orientation, significantly influenced his work later in life. The impact of being a minority translated well into his writing and helped spawn one of the most important plays in a generation.

Kushner's play *Angels in America* was a seven-and-a-half-hour, two-day play that went against all the theater conventions of the time. The production was divided into two parts (*Angels in America: Millennium Approaches* and *Angels in America: Perestroika*) and placed a minority group at the center of history. It allowed the American theater-going public to witness a gay storyline as a human one; a story full of love, loss, denial, rejection, survival, intersectionality, and the power of community. It was also one of the first major theatrical works to tackle the subject of AIDS in a way that engaged broad audiences. Kushner won numerous awards for *Angels in America*, including a Pulitzer Prize and two back-to-back Tony Awards, one in 1993 for *Millennium Approaches* and the other in 1994 for *Perestroika*. In 2003, the play was adapted into a miniseries for HBO starring Al Pacino, Meryl Streep, and Emma Thompson. The television version won several Emmy Awards and Golden Globes. The play was revived on Broadway in 2018, with Andrew Garfield and Nathan Lane both winning Tony Awards for their performances.

After *Angels in America* catapulted Kushner into stardom, he went on to write numerous other projects including *Caroline, or Change*, a 2004 musical about a maid and the changes she, and those around her, go through during the American civil rights movement. Kushner took on Hollywood, teaming up with Eric Roth to co-write the award-winning screenplay for Steven Spielberg's 2005 film, *Munich*, starring Eric Bana and Daniel Craig. He later joined Spielberg again on the screenplay for the award-winning 2012 film *Lincoln*, starring Daniel Day-Lewis. *Lincoln* grossed over $275 million at the box office and was nominated for twelve Academy Awards, more than any other film that year. Other collaborations with Spielberg include *West Side Story* (2021) and *The Fabelmans* (2022).

Kushner is an intellectually robust and prolific writer with the capacity to emotionally connect audiences to historic moments in time. Whether on stage or on screen, his scripts have captivated viewers across the globe. That's why President Obama presented him with the 2012 National Medal of Arts. When it comes to American theater and film, Kushner is an American treasure.

Acknowledgments

We would like to take the opportunity to thank the following people who helped us with this project.

First, and foremost, thank you to our spouses for supporting us through this journey. You were our extra pair of eyes, our cheerleaders, and our therapists. We couldn't have done this without you.

Thank you to Stephen Alexander for helping us with initial proofreading of some of the earlier profiles. Your insight was extremely valuable.

Thank you to our editor, Brenda Knight, for keeping us on track and encouraging us along the way.

Michael Bedwell, thank you for providing feedback on the profile for Leonard P. Matlovich and for keeping his spirit alive through www.leonardmatlovich.com.

Thank you to Robin Miller, Megan Werner, Anna de la O, and the entire team at Mango Publishing who helped navigate this project through all phases of production, cover design, editing, formatting, marketing, distribution, and more. You helped make this book a reality and we are forever grateful for your support!

About the Authors

Eric Rosswood is an award-winning author, activist, and commentator on LGBTQ+ issues, including civil rights, parenting, marriage, and politics. He writes books that celebrate and honor queer joy, from adult books like *The Ultimate Guide for Gay Dads*, to teen books like *Queer Cheer* and stories for younger children like the Stonewall Honor award-winning picture book, *STRONG*. When not writing, Eric enjoys spending time with his family, watching movies, reading, and traveling to exciting places around the world.

Kathleen Archambeau is an award-winning writer and longtime LGBTQ+ activist. A native San Franciscan, she was a founding contributor to the James Hormel LGBTQ+ wing of the San Francisco Public Library. As Vice President and Co-Chair of the Fundraising Committee of the Board of Directors of Operation Concern, one of the oldest and largest mental health agencies serving the LGBTQ+ community, she was given an Outstanding Service Award. With her Kiwi wife, Kathleen Archambeau competed and won two Bronze Medals in Ballroom Dancing at the Gay Games in Cologne, Germany. Archambeau contributed a regular column profiling LGBTQ+ artists in one of the longest-running LGBTQ+ publications in the US, *The San Francisco Bay Times*. Archambeau's first book, *Climbing the Corporate Ladder in High Heels*, was featured in *Forbes* twice, endorsed by US House of Representatives Majority Leader Nancy Pelosi and CEO and Chair of BareEssentuals, Leslie Blodgett, and translated into Chinese, Korean, Lithuanian, and Portuguese. She is proud to have been the co-author on the original edition of this book, titled *We Make It Better*, published in 2019. Her essay, "Seized," one of only two lesbian creative nonfiction entries in a collection of twenty-one authors entitled, *The Other Woman*, edited by Victoria Zackheim, was lauded by *Publishers Weekly* for its "...top-drawer writers." Archambeau serves on the Board of the Women's National Book Association—SF Chapter. Kathleen Archambeau was a Department of Education Fellow at the University of Iowa and is a legacy donor focused on LGBTQ+ writers to the University of Iowa Writers Workshop. Archambeau served as an LGBTQ+ Elder in the Swig Program in Jewish Studies and Social Justice at the University of San Francisco where she had previously taught for twelve years. She and her wife appeared in The Trevor Project video series aimed at preventing LGBTQ+ suicide, "Come Dance With Us," directed by Robert Cortlandt and Winter Held. She lives with her wife and Guide Dog Career Change Puppy in the San Francisco Bay Area.

Resources

All links active at time of publication.

Introduction

https://ilga.org/downloads/2017/ILGA_State_Sponsored_
Homophobia_2017_WEB.pdf

https://www.counseling.org/news/aca-blogs/aca-government-affairs-blog/
aca-government-affairs-blog/2018/05/31/conversion-therapy-bans-become-
law-in-three-more-states

https://williamsinstitute.law.ucla.edu/press/conversion-therapy-release/

Marsha P. Johnson and Sylvia Rivera

https://www.biography.com/activists/marsha-p-johnson-sylvia-
rivera-friendship

https://www.biography.com/activists/marsha-p-johnson

https://www.biography.com/activists/sylvia-rivera

https://www.womenshistory.org/education-resources/biographies/
marsha-p-johnson

https://wams.nyhistory.org/growth-and-turmoil/growing-tensions/
marsha-p-johnson/

https://www.si.edu/stories/marsha-johnson-sylvia-rivera-and-
history-pride-month

https://gaycitynews.com/exploding-the-myths-of-stonewall/

https://www.nps.gov/people/marsha-p-johnson.htm

https://www.nps.gov/people/sylvia-rivera.htm

https://www.nps.gov/articles/000/marsha-p-johnson-sylvia-rivera.htm

https://www.insideedition.com/the-death-of-marsha-p-johnson-and-the-
quest-for-closure-51708

https://www.metroweekly.com/2020/08/new-york-governor-dedicates-state-park-in-memory-of-lgbtq-activist-marsha-p-johnson/

https://www.advocate.com/transgender/2015/10/27/sylvia-rivera-gets-place-national-portrait-gallery

https://www.brooklynpaper.com/marsha-p-johnson-park-new-gateway-reno/

https://www.parks.ny.gov/parks/155

Kelley Robinson

https://www.hrc.org/campaigns/national-state-of-emergency-for-lgbtq-americans

https://www.hrc.org/about/staff/kelley-robinson

https://www.hrc.org/about

https://www.msnbc.com/the-last-word/watch/robinson-respect-for-marriage-act-an-important-step-in-journey-to-freedom-and-equality-156040261904

https://brenebrown.com/articles/2024/05/13/5-questions-with-kelley-robinson/

https://www.hrc.org/press-releases/kelley-robinson-president-of-the-human-rights-campaign-named-on-the-time-list-of-the-100-most-influential-people-in-the-world

https://www.hrc.org/press-releases/kelley-robinson-to-serve-as-president-of-the-human-rights-campaign

https://www.youtube.com/watch?v=m1B9zlGMzHo

https://time.com/6964843/kelley-robinson/

https://www.youtube.com/watch?v=oKpLuaeLPCQ

https://www.americanprogressaction.org/article/kelley-robinson-says-were-here-were-queer-and-we-are-voting/

https://www.advocate.com/news/2022/9/20/kelley-robinson-black-queer-woman-new-human-rights-campaign-head

https://www.hrc.org/press-releases/human-rights-campaign-joins-president-biden-in-endorsing-kamala-harris-for-president

Bayard Rustin

https://obamawhitehouse.archives.gov/the-press-office/2013/11/20/remarks-president-presidential-medal-freedom-ceremony

https://www.glsen.org/blog/black-history-month-heroes-bayard-rustin

https://www.britannica.com/biography/Bayard-Rustin

https://aflcio.org/about/history/labor-history-people/bayard-rustin

http://www.pbs.org/wnet/african-americans-many-rivers-to-cross/history/100-amazing-facts/who-designed-the-march-on-washington/

https://www.biography.com/people/bayard-rustin-9467932

https://www.americanprogress.org/issues/lgbt/reports/2013/08/23/72807/lessons-from-bayard-rustin-why-economic-justice-is-an-lgbt-issue/

https://www.psychologytoday.com/us/blog/the-sexual-continuum/201201/bayard-rustin-forgotten-civil-rights-hero

https://www.history.com/topics/black-history/march-on-washington

http://www.crmvet.org/docs/moworg2.pdf

https://www.dol.gov/general/aboutdol/hallofhonor/2013_rustin

X González

https://www.harpersbazaar.com/culture/politics/a18715714/protesting-nra-gun-control-true-story/

https://www.newyorker.com/news/news-desk/three-days-in-parkland-florida

https://www.washingtonpost.com/news/post-nation/wp/2018/03/01/emma-gonzalez-la-nueva-cara-of-florida-latinx

https://people.com/crime/parkland-shooting-survivor-emma-gonzalez-more-twitter-followers-nra/

https://www.cnn.com/2018/03/25/us/emma-gonzalez-what-you-need-to-know-trnd/index.html

http://www.foxnews.com/us/2018/02/14/florida-school-shooting-among-10-deadliest-in-modern-us-history.html https://www.theguardian.com/us-news/ng-interactive/2017/oct/02/america-mass-shootings-gun-violence

https://www.nytimes.com/2018/02/18/us/emma-gonzalez-florida-shooting.html

https://www.cnn.com/2018/03/09/us/florida-gov-scott-gun-bill/index.html

http://www.newsweek.com/march-our-lives-how-many-2-million-90-voting-district-860841

Nyle DiMarco

https://www.gallaudet.edu/news/nyle_dimarco_antm

https://www.washingtonpost.com/lifestyle/style/own-your-identity-the-first-deaf-contestant-on-americas-next-top-model/2015/08/07/6ef1d3b4-39f1-11e5-8e98-115a3cf7d7ae_story.html

https://news.wisc.edu/deaf-actor-activist-nyle-dimarco-connects-with-deaf-students-in-intimate-qa-session/

https://wfdeaf.org/our-work/

https://news.un.org/en/story/2018/09/1019922

https://twitter.com/NyleDiMarco/status/647398826349850624

http://time.com/4301926/dancing-with-the-stars-nyle-dimarco/

https://attitude.co.uk/article/watch-nyle-dimarco-accept-attitudes-man-of-the-year-award-supported-by-virgin-holidays/16108/

Cecelia Maria Zarbo Wambach, PhD

http://ceceliawambach.com/my-life-bio/

https://www.sfgate.com/news/article/Schools-get-1-4-million-from-Hewlett-Annenberg-3138730.php

https://www.linkedin.com/in/wambach-cecelia-85a27245/

https://www.imdb.com/name/nm9048940/

https://refugeeeducationandlearning.org/

https://refugeeeducationandlearning.org/volunteers

https://refugeeeducationandlearning.org/girls-empowerment

https://refugeeeducationandlearning.org/team/

https://www.sfchronicle.com/bayarea/article/East-Bay-retirees-volunteer-in-Greece-with-13001205.php

https://www.sfgate.com/bayarea/article/Bay-Area-educators-reinvent-retirement-on-a-Greek-12980097.php

https://www.unicef.org/eca/press-releases/greece-back-school-refugee-migrant-children

https://www.sfgate.com/opinion/article/EDITORIAL-Teaching-the-Teachers-On-the-job-2850206.php

http://ceceliawambach.com/my-life-bio

Beth Ford

https://www.linkedin.com/feed/update/urn:li:activity:6437698781155770368/

https://www.linkedin.com/pulse/welcome-family-vermont-creamery-beth-ford/

https://www.linkedin.com/pulse/shared-holiday-favorite-beth-ford/

https://www.linkedin.com/pulse/privilege-fulfilling-our-community-commitment-beth-ford/

https://www.linkedin.com/pulse/5-essential-life-hacks-driving-global-business-beth-ford/

https://www.businessinsider.com/beth-ford-land-o-lakes-ceo-2018-7

https://www.landolakesinc.com/Press/News/beth-ford-named-ceo

http://fortune.com/2018/07/26/land-o-lakes-beth-ford-ceo/

https://www.advocate.com/business/2018/7/30/land-olakes-beth-ford-becomes-first-out-woman-run-fortune-500

https://www.bloomberg.com/profiles/people/3598807-beth-e-ford

https://www.huffingtonpost.com/entry/beth-ford-land-olakes-gay-ceo_us_5b5f3004e4b0de86f49966d5

https://www.wsj.com/articles/land-olakes-names-next-ceo-1532611476

http://fortune.com/most-powerful-women/beth-ford-30/

https://www.cnn.com/2018/10/01/business/land-o-lakes-beth-ford/index.html

http://fortune.com/2018/10/02/beth-ford-land-o-lakes/

http://fortune.com/2018/07/26/land-o-lakes-beth-ford-ceo/

https://www.landolakesinc.com/Press/News/beth-ford-named-ceo

http://time.com/money/5409815/land-o-lakes-ceo-beth-ford-career-advice/

https://www.bloomberg.com/research/stocks/private/person.
asp?personId=506682

https://www.hrc.org/resources/the-cost-of-the-closet-and-the-
rewards-of-inclusion

Rick Welts

https://www.youtube.com/watch?v=e6SR3XyOIqU

https://www.nba.com/warriors/staff/rick-welts

https://www.seattletimes.com/sports/nba/rick-welts-remarkable-journey-from-
sonics-ball-boy-to-basketball-hall-of-fame/

https://www.nbcsports.com/bayarea/warriors/rick-welts-hall-fame-personality-
deserves-much-praise-anyone

https://abc7news.com/sports/warriors-president-rick-welts-on-being-
inducted-to-nba-hall-of-fame/4186486/

https://www.bloomberg.com/research/stocks/private/person.
asp?personId=34075339

https://www.symphonicsource.com/blog/11-quotes-on-building-a-
championship-culture-from-the-golden-state-warriors/

https://www.sportsbusinessdaily.com/Daily/Issues/1997/10/21/Leagues-
Governing-Bodies/BRANDWEEK-HONORS-WNBAS-ACKERMAN-AND-
WELTS-AS-TOP-MARKETERS.aspx

http://www.youcanplayproject.org/pages/staff-and-board

http://www.nba.com/video/2018/09/07/20180907-hall-fame-
rick-welts-speech

https://www.nba.com/warriors/news/hof-2018-class-announcement-20180331

Suze Orman

https://www.youtube.com/watch?v=GTN9HyOVsUY&feature=youtu.be

https://www.thehotline.org/women-breaking-free

https://www.suzeorman.com/resources

https://www.cnbc.com/video/2018/10/12/suze-orman-you-dont-need-to-buy-a-home-to-be-financially-secure.html

https://www.suzeorman.com/about-suze/tv-radio

https://www.suzeorman.com/products

https://money.cnn.com/2014/11/25/media/new-suze-orman-show/index.html

https://www.businessinsider.com/suze-orman-is-leaving-cnbc-2014-11

http://time.com/money/4989311/retire-like-suze-2/

https://awakenthegreatnesswithin.com/40-inspirational-suze-orman-quotes-on-success/

http://content.time.com/time/specials/2007/article/0,28804,1733748_1733752_1736278,00.html

http://content.time.com/time/specials/packages/article/0,28804,1984685_1985123_1985086,00.html

https://www.usnews.com/news/blogs/washington-whispers/2008/10/07/suze-ormans-coming-out-at-the-human-rights-campaign-dinner

https://www.military.com/daily-news/2017/01/04/suze-orman-give-soldiers-free-money-education-course.html

https://corporate.discovery.com/discovery-newsroom/suze-orman-at-the-apollo-women-and-money-special-to-air-exclusively-on-own-monday-october-1/

https://www.hrc.org/blog/video-suze-orman-on-how-doma-hurts-the-american-economy

https://www.afterellen.com/tv/5276-suze-orman-comes-out-2

https://www.nytimes.com/2007/02/25/magazine/25wwlnq4.t.html

https://people.com/tv/suze-orman-talks-rags-riches-rise-finding-soulmate-age-50/

Tim Cook

https://www.bloomberg.com/news/articles/2014-10-30/tim-cook-speaks-up

http://time.com/4036006/tim-cook-coming-out-gay/

https://www.cnbc.com/2017/11/06/tim-cooks-performance-as-apple-ceo-profits-sales-and-innovation.html

https://www.cnbc.com/2015/03/26/apples-tim-cook-will-give-away-all-his-money.html

https://www.nytimes.com/interactive/2017/12/05/your-money/apple-market-share.html

https://www.fastcompany.com/3062090/playing-the-long-game-inside-tim-cooks-apple

https://www.investopedia.com/insights/what-makes-aapl-valuable-company/

https://www.statista.com/statistics/273439/number-of-employees-of-apple-since-2005/

https://www.inc.com/business-insider/best-quotes-tim-cook.html

http://fortune.com/2017/04/17/apple-ceo-tim-cook-lgbt-free-speech/

https://www.usatoday.com/story/money/2015/03/06/379-companies-want-gay-marriage-bans-overturned/24486461/

https://www.newsweek.com/apple-ceo-tim-cook-shares-tech-giants-plan-fight-racism-after-trumps-651763

https://www.usatoday.com/story/tech/news/2017/02/06/97-tech-firms-file-court-brief-opposing-immigration-ban/97538208/

https://www.wsj.com/articles/workplace-equality-is-good-for-business-1383522254

https://www.telegraph.co.uk/technology/apple/10424816/Apple-CEO-Tim-Cook-speaks-out-for-gay-rights-in-the-workplace.html

https://www.wired.com/2015/07/apple-equality-act/

https://www.wired.com/2015/03/tim-cook-religious-freedom-laws/

https://www.imore.com/history-iphone-original

https://www.usatoday.com/story/money/2018/08/02/apple-first-stock-hit-1-trillion-market-value/877867002/

Frida Kahlo

https://www.britannica.com/biography/Frida-Kahlo

https://www.biography.com/artists/frida-kahlo

https://www.smithsonianmag.com/arts-culture/frida-kahlo-70745811/

https://www.moma.org/artists/2963

https://www.smithsonianmag.com/smart-news/frida-kahlos-intimate-self-portrait-sells-for-record-high-price-180979082/

https://www.liberationnews.org/five-things-to-know-about-frida-kahlo-the-communist/

https://www.biography.com/artists/frida-kahlo-real-rumored-affairs-men-women

https://nmwa.org/art/artists/frida-kahlo/

https://www.kqed.org/news/11710877/san-francisco-unveils-frida-kahlo-way-renaming-phelan-avenue

https://www.pbs.org/show/becoming-frida-kahlo/

Bill T. Jones

http://newyorklivearts.org/download/BTJ_FULL_BIO.pdf

https://www.broadwayworld.com/article/2010-Tony-Awards-Bill-T-Jones-Wins-Best-Choreography-20100613

https://www.nytimes.com/2015/06/20/arts/dance/review-bill-t-jones-arnie-zane-summons-a-life-during-wartime.html

https://www.nytimes.com/2007/06/07/arts/dance/07jone.html

http://www.pbs.org/black-culture/shows/list/bill-t-jones-a-good-man/

http://www.pbs.org/wnet/americanmasters/bill-t-jones-a-good-man-biographical-essay-and-tribute/1895/

http://www.kennedy-center.org/artist/A4338

https://www.arts.gov/honors/medals/bill-t-jones

http://content.time.com/time/covers/0,16641,19941010,00.html

https://www.nytimes.com/2016/06/06/t-magazine/bill-t-jones-dance-choreography.html

Jin Xing

https://www.youtube.com/watch?v=IC01XrgzZ7w

http://usa.chinadaily.com.cn/china/2015-10/17/content_22205398.htm

http://www.scmp.com/news/china/society/article/2087720/how-transgender-dancer-jin-xing-conquered-chinese-tv

https://www.pri.org/stories/2015-06-03/10-transgender-icons-around-world-who-should-be-famous-caitlyn-jenner

https://www.hollywoodreporter.com/features/meet-oprah-china-who-happens-be-transgender-942750

https://www.glaad.org/blog/glaad-global-voices-trans-chinese-dancer-does-it-all?response_type=embed

https://www.economist.com/china/2017/02/11/chinas-transgender-oprah

https://www.huffingtonpost.com/2015/04/09/jin-xing-transgender-china_n_7034270.html

https://www.nytimes.com/1999/09/14/world/beijing-journal-as-china-changes-a-sex-change-can-bring-fame.html

https://www.cnn.com/2013/07/11/world/asia/china-jin-xing-sex-change/index.html

https://www.newsweek.com/once-male-soldier-now-female-dancer-china-66057

RuPaul

https://www.emmys.com/shows/rupauls-drag-race

https://www.biography.com/celebrities/rupaul

https://www.cnn.com/2021/09/19/entertainment/rupaul-emmys/index.html

https://walkoffame.com/rupaul-andre-charles/

https://www.emmys.com/bios/rupaul-charles

https://variety.com/2024/tv/news/rupaul-most-awarded-host-reality-competition-drag-race-emmys-2024-1235863721/

https://ew.com/emmys-most-nominated-hosts-rupaul-heidi-klum-tom-bergeron-8679507

https://www.cbsnews.com/news/rupaul-emmy-drag-queen-story-hours-rupauls-drag-race/

Hannah Gadsby

https://www.nytimes.com/2018/07/24/arts/hannah-gadsby-comedy-nanette.html

https://www.theguardian.com/stage/2022/mar/19/hannah-gadsby-autism-diagnosis-little-out-of-whack

https://www.npr.org/2020/05/26/862081893/autism-spectrum-diagnosis-helped-comic-hannah-gadsby-be-kinder-to-herself

https://peabodyawards.com/award-profile/hannah-gadsby-nanette/

https://deadline.com/2019/04/peabody-awards-barry-killing-eve-hannah-gadsby-pose-entertainment-winners-list-1202598447/

https://theconversation.com/hannah-gadsby-navigates-the-mirror-maze-of-trauma-as-an-autistic-gender-queer-comedian-176010

https://www.rollingstone.com/tv-movies/tv-movie-features/hannah-gadsby-interview-something-special-netflix-ted-sarandos-dave-chappelle-queer-joy-transgender-rights-1234732285/

https://people.com/tv/comedian-hannah-gadbsy-reveals-she-got-married-in-january/

https://people.com/who-is-jenney-shamash-hannah-gadsby-wife-8600639

Ariana DeBose

https://www.biography.com/actors/ariana-debose

https://www.imdb.com/name/nm3663196/bio/

https://www.britannica.com/biography/Ariana-DeBose

https://www.aclu.org/bio/ariana-debose

https://unitedarts.org/wp-content/uploads/2021/01/Ariana-DeBose-Biography-1.pdf

https://glaad.org/ariana-debose-makes-history-and-more-lgbtq-moments-94th-annual-academy-awards/

https://m.playbill.com/person/ariana-debose-vault-0000123224

https://goldenglobes.com/person/ariana-debose/

https://nypost.com/2021/12/08/west-side-story-star-ariana-debose-dazzles-as-anita/

https://www.newsobserver.com/entertainment/article259737975.html

https://broadwaydirect.com/how-ariana-debose-went-from-broadway-to-hollywood-in-the-prom-on-netflix/

https://www.detroitnews.com/story/entertainment/2021/12/30/ariana-debose-talks-her-life-changing-role-west-side-story/9045276002/

Daniela Vega

http://remezcla.com/features/film/daniela-vega-a-fantastic-woman/

https://www.theguardian.com/film/2018/mar/01/a-fantastic-woman-review-sebastian-lelio-daniela-vega

https://www.theguardian.com/film/2018/feb/18/daniela-vega-transgender-star-film-industry-a-fantastic-woman-interview

https://www.backstage.com/interview/daniela-vegas-winding-path-acting/

http://time.com/collection-post/5217558/daniela-vega/

http://time.com/collection/most-influential-people-2018/5217558/daniela-vega/

https://www.vice.com/en_us/article/a3795k/an-oscar-nomination-for-daniela-vega-would-make-trans-hollywood-history

https://www.bbc.com/news/world-latin-america-43320379

http://time.com/5186869/daniela-vega-oscars-2018/

http://www.latimes.com/entertainment/movies/la-et-mn-daniela-vega-20171113-htmlstory.html

https://www.wmagazine.com/story/daniela-vega-transgender-actress-oscar-nomination

https://www.harpersbazaar.com/culture/film-tv/a19057004/who-is-daniela-vega-oscars-2018-a-fantastic-woman-nominee/

https://www.nbcnews.com/feature/nbc-out/first-fantastic-woman-wins-oscar-transgender-lead-n853626

https://twitter.com/mbachelet/status/970485105549561856

Robin Roberts

https://www.biography.com/people/robin-roberts-21188247

https://abcnews.go.com/GMA/robin-roberts-biography/story?id=128237

https://rtdna.org/article/rtdnf_announces_2018_first_amendment_award_honorees

http://www.peabodyawards.com/award-profile/robins-journey

https://www.cnn.com/2013/12/29/showbiz/robin-roberts-comes-out

https://abcnews.go.com/GMA/robin-roberts-reports-pass-christian-mississippi-years-hurricane/story?id=11493018

Roberts, *My Story, My Song: Mother-Daughter Reflections on Life and Faith*, Nashville, TN: Upper Room Books, 2012.

Roberts, Robin, *From the Heart: 8 Rules to Live By,* NYC, NY: Hyperion, 2008.

Roberts, Robin, with Veronica Chambers, *Everybody's Got Something*, NYC, NY: Grand Central Publishing, Hachette Book Group, 2014.

https://www.youtube.com/watch?v=vJyCl2uE_cE

https://www.youtube.com/watch?v=7lscELxqihs

https://www.youtube.com/watch?v=AjQf_DBToXA

https://www.youtube.com/watch?v=kQGMTPab9GQ

https://www.youtube.com/watch?v=3TmcB8Bzl38

https://www.youtube.com/watch?v=d0uOoaw21l0

Chris Nee

http://www.peabodyawards.com/award-profile/doc-mcstuffins

https://www.imdb.com/name/nm1349008/awards?ref_=nm_awd

https://variety.com/2015/tv/news/michelle-obama-doc-mcstuffins-1201601593/

https://www.adweek.com/tv-video/disney-wraps-major-upfront-sales-150977/

http://time.com/3079446/disneys-perfect-answer-to-barbie-is-doc-mcstuffins/

https://www.nytimes.com/2014/07/27/business/a-disney-doctor-speaks-of-identity-to-little-girls.html

https://www.workingmother.com/content/chris-nee-disney-junior-doc-mcstuffins

https://www.huffingtonpost.com/author/chris-nee

https://www.glaad.org/blog/how-disney-teaching-valuable-family-lessons-episode-doc-mcstuffins-featuring-wanda-sykes-and

https://www.wired.com/2012/05/doc-mcstuffins-and-writer-producer-chris-nee/

https://thegrio.com/2013/09/30/doc-mcstuffins-creator-explains-why-shows-lead-character-is-black/

Sir Ian McKellen

http://www.bbc.co.uk/bbcthree/article/70b15fcd-3e98-4ce0-a192-5f4b78212ae9

https://www.britannica.com/biography/Ian-McKellen

http://mckellen.com

https://www.stonewall.org.uk/people/ian-mckellen

https://www.biography.com/people/ian-mckellen-9392833

Margaret Cho

https://www.nytimes.com/2014/12/25/us/with-memories-of-a-comic-comrade-margaret-cho-helps-the-homeless.html

https://www.huffingtonpost.com/entry/margaret-cho-bisexuality-pride_us_5b27b980e4b0783ae12b754e

http://news.berkeley.edu/2018/03/22/front-row-with-margaret-cho-and-friends/

https://www.biography.com/people/margaret-cho-20984631

https://www.rollingstone.com/culture/culture-lists/50-best-stand-up-comics-of-all-time-126359/margaret-cho-3-126676/

https://www.npr.org/2011/05/31/136818644/margaret-cho-breaks-barriers-in-world-of-comedy

https://www.fandango.com/people/margaret-cho-116276/biography

https://archives.sfweekly.com/thesnitch/2008/05/01/last-night-margaret-cho-day-at-city-hall

https://www.tvguide.com/celebrities/margaret-cho/bio/163864/

https://www.washingtonpost.com/express/wp/2017/10/13/post-rehab-margaret-cho-has-come-back-to-life-for-her-fresh-off-the-bloat-tour/

http://www.jademagazine.com/Ad_sample_large.html

http://www.pbs.org/wnet/pioneers-of-television/pioneering-people/margaret-cho/

The Wachowskis

https://www.loc.gov/item/prn-12-226/cinematic-firsts-enshrined-in-2012-film-registry/2012-12-19/

https://www.biography.com/people/lana-wachowski-21095557

https://www.biography.com/people/lilly-wachowski-21095529

http://www.imdb.com/title/tt0133093/awards

http://www.imdb.com/name/nm0905154/bio?ref_=nm_ov_bio_sm

https://www.huffingtonpost.com/2012/07/30/matrix-director-sex-change-larry-wachowski_n_1720944.html

http://people.com/movies/lilly-lana-wachowski-how-transgender-siblings-supported-each-other/

Harvey Milk

https://www.biography.com/political-figures/harvey-milk

https://milkfoundation.org/about/harvey-milk-biography

https://www.ebar.com/story.php?id=288094

https://www.navytimes.com/news/your-navy/2021/11/07/navy-launches-ship-named-for-gay-rights-leader-harvey-milk/

https://www.sfgate.com/travel/article/Harvey-Milk-Terminal-1-first-look-pictures-sf-14047873.php

https://www.flysfo.com/hmt1

https://daily.jstor.org/harvey-milks-gay-freedom-day-speech-annotated/

https://voicesofdemocracy.umd.edu/milk-youve-got-to-have-hope-speech-text/

https://www.nytimes.com/2022/05/25/arts/music/harvey-milk-opera.html

https://obamawhitehouse.archives.gov/blog/2014/05/22/harvey-milk-forever-stamp-dedicated

https://obamawhitehouse.archives.gov/the-press-office/president-obama-names-medal-freedom-recipients

Mary Yu

https://ballotpedia.org/Mary_Yu

https://www.seattletimes.com/seattle-news/justice-mary-yu-on-marriage-and-adoptions-for-all-seattle-pride-at-50/

https://www.courts.wa.gov/appellate_trial_courts/supreme/bios/?fa=scbios.display_file&fileID=yu

https://law.seattleu.edu/faculty/directory/profiles/yu-justice-mary-i.html

https://www.thestranger.com/blogs/2012/12/08/15483647/whos-marrying-the-first-gay-couple-judge-mary-yu

https://justicemaryyu.com

Pete Buttigieg

https://www.transportation.gov/meet-secretary/secretary-pete-buttigieg

https://www.southbendtribune.com/story/news/local/2015/06/16/south-bend-mayor-why-coming-out-matters/45761773/

https://www.britannica.com/biography/Pete-Buttigieg

https://www.biography.com/political-figures/pete-buttigieg

https://kids.britannica.com/students/article/Pete-Buttigieg/633205

https://time.com/collection/time-100-next-2019/5718831/pete-buttigieg/

https://southbendin.gov/wp-content/uploads/2018/05/Code_FinalVATF_Report_2_red.pdf

https://www.southbendtribune.com/story/news/local/2019/04/13/what-now-for-south-bend-neighborhoods-after-1000-houses-in-1000-days/117179140/

https://www.953mnc.com/2020/09/28/south-bend-mayor-james-mueller-got-married-this-weekend/

https://www.in.gov/library/files/HPI150625.pdf

https://www.nytimes.com/2013/12/21/automobiles/south-bend-ind-to-recall-studebakers-1963-departure.html

https://www.huduser.gov/portal/pdredge/pdr-edge-inpractice-011116.html

Jóhanna Sigurðardóttir

https://www.forbes.com/lists/2009/11/power-women-09_The-100-Most-Powerful-Women_Rank_3.html

http://news.bbc.co.uk/2/hi/europe/7863923.stm

http://www.bbc.com/news/business-11517459

http://www.nordiclabourjournal.org/artikler/portrett/portrait-2012/article.2012-03-07.7696496692 https://www.newstatesman.com/international-politics/2010/01/iceland-interview-economy

https://www.telegraph.co.uk/women/womens-politics/10756847/Icelands-Jonina-Leosdottir-I-was-the-worlds-first-lesbian-First-Lady.html

Leo Varadkar

http://leovaradkar.ie/

https://www.theguardian.com/commentisfree/2017/jun/04/gay-irish-prime-minister-leo-varadkar-fine-gael-taoiseach

https://www.brookings.edu/events/ireland-in-europe-and-the-world-a-conversation-with-irish-taoiseach-leo-varadkar/

https://www.straitstimes.com/world/united-states/irelands-prime-minister-leo-varadkar-defends-undocumented-irish-immigrants

http://www.irishhealth.com/article.html?id=25270

https://www.irishtimes.com/news/politics/varadkar-backs-yes-vote-saying-ireland-should-trust-women-and-trust-doctors-1.3469913

https://www.bbc.com/news/world-europe-40134140

https://www.taoiseach.gov.ie/eng/Taoiseach_and_Government/About_the_Taoiseach/

https://www.britannica.com/biography/Leo-Varadkar

https://www.washingtonpost.com/world/europe/ireland-votes-to-repeal-its-ban-on-abortion/2018/05/26/fb675fa8-603b-11e8-b656-236c6214ef01_story.html

https://www.irishtimes.com/news/social-affairs/why-did-varadkar-change-his-mind-on-abortion-1.3373470

https://www.independent.co.uk/voices/ireland-abortion-referendum-illegal-legal-rape-vote-may-june-2018-20-december-decision-a8110706.html

https://www.bbc.com/news/world-europe-45568094

https://www.nbcnews.com/feature/nbc-out/ireland-appears-set-elect-first-openly-gay-prime-minister-n765426

https://www.theguardian.com/world/2017/jun/02/leo-varadkar-becomes-irelands-prime-minister-elect https://www.huffingtonpost.com/entry/leo-varadkar-st-patricks-day-parade_us_5aafc8b7e4b0697dfe18b442

https://www.irishtimes.com/news/politics/leo-varadkar-i-am-a-gay-man-minister-says-1.2070189

Eric Fanning

https://www.defense.gov/About/Biographies/Biography-View/article/778714/eric-fanning/

https://www.cbsnews.com/news/a-final-salute-to-eric-fanning/

http://www.washingtonblade.com/2013/04/19/senate-confirms-gay-official-as-air-force-under-secretary/

https://www.washingtontimes.com/news/2016/jun/20/troops-welcome-eric-fanning-army-secretary-with-fa/

https://www.army.mil/article/174964/americas_diversity_is_our_armys_strength

Technical Sergeant Leonard P. Matlovich

http://time.com/4019076/40-years-leonard-matlovich/

http://www.leonardmatlovich.com

https://www.nytimes.com/1988/06/24/us/gay-airman-who-fought-ouster-dies-from-aids.html

https://lgbthistorymonth.com/leonard-matlovich?tab=biography

https://www.airforcetimes.com/news/your-air-force/2015/11/14/on-veterans-day-lgbt-troops-honor-two-of-their-own/

https://www.huffingtonpost.com/jennifer-bendery/leonard-matlovich-gay-veteran_b_6141746.html

Brandi Carlile

https://www.npr.org/transcripts/983815671

https://www.npr.org/2021/10/08/1044006453

https://people.com/parents/grammys-2023-brandi-carlile-wife-daughters-introduce-her-performance/

https://variety.com/2021/music/reviews/brandi-carlile-broken-horses-memoir-book-review-1234945395/

https://americansongwriter.com/4-songs-you-didnt-know-twins-phil-and-tim-hanseroth-wrote-for-brandi-carlile/

https://www.encyclopedia.com/education/news-wires-white-papers-and-books/carlile-brandi

https://parade.com/1361531/radhika-menon/brandi-carlile-wife-catherine-shepherd/

https://www.nytimes.com/2021/04/01/arts/music/brandi-carlile-broken-horses.html

https://www.iheart.com/podcast/990-broken-record-with-rick-ru-28643863/episode/brandi-carlile-and-tish-melton-162196852/

https://www.lookingoutfoundation.org/

Sir Elton John

https://www.biography.com/people/elton-john-9355335

https://www.rollingstone.com/music/artists/elton-john/biography

http://www.guinnessworldrecords.com/world-records/59721-best-selling-single

https://www.billboard.com/articles/columns/chart-beat/5557800/hot-100-55th-anniversary-by-the-numbers-top-100-artists-most-no

https://www.eltonjohn.com/charities

https://www.nytimes.com/2014/11/30/fashion/elton-john-and-darren-walker-on-race-sexual-identity-and-leaving-the-past-behind.html

k.d. lang

https://www.biography.com/people/kd-lang-21174577

https://www.canadaswalkoffame.com/inductees/2008/kd-lang

https://www.grammy.com/grammys/artists/kd-lang

https://www.cbc.ca/news/canada/calgary/kd-lang-fashion-cowboy-bride-coming-out-1.3657007

https://www.nytimes.com/2018/03/22/style/kd-lang-ingenue-tour.html

https://www.washingtonpost.com/archive/lifestyle/1990/07/02/cattle-countrys-beef-with-kd-lang/7dd680b4-ecf0-407a-aed5-b6120b879d38/

https://junoawards.ca/nomination/2013-canadian-music-hall-of-fame-k-d-lang/

http://www.vh1.com/news/1238/the-100-greatest-women-in-music/

https://celebrityaccess.com/caarchive/cmt-reveals-its-list-of-40-greatest-women-in-country-music/

Leonard Bernstein

http://www.classicfm.com/composers/bernstein-l/guides/leonard-bernstein-quotes/

https://leonardbernstein.com/resources/press-room/leonard-bernstein-at-100

https://www.prospectmagazine.co.uk/magazine/leonard-bernstein-invented-how-we-do-modern-classical-music

http://www.interlude.hk/front/leonard-bernstein-felicia-montealegrea-divided-life/

http://www.sfsymphony.org/Watch-Listen-Learn/Read-Program-Notes/Articles-Interviews/My-father-Leonard-Bernstein

http://www.sfsymphony.org/Watch-Listen-Learn/Read-Program-Notes/Articles-Interviews/The-Best-of-All-Possible-Worlds

https://www.biography.com/people/leonard-bernstein-9210269

https://www.britannica.com/biography/Leonard-Bernstein

https://www.npr.org/sections/deceptivecadence/2018/08/25/638625561/life-with-leonard-bernstein

https://nyphil.org/jfk

https://www.whitehousehistory.org/leonard-bernstein-at-the-kennedy-white-house

https://www.loc.gov/item/2010646104/

http://www.praemiumimperiale.org/en/laureate-en/music-en/bernstein-en

http://www.theaterhalloffame.org/members.html#B

https://www.colorado.edu/event/bernstein/leonard-bernstein/accolades

https://www.grammy.com/grammys/artists/leonard-bernstein

Ricky Martin

https://www.biography.com/people/ricky-martin-9542230

https://www.grammy.com/grammys/artists/ricky-martin

http://www.walkoffame.com/ricky-martin

https://www.unicef.org/people/people_51425.html

https://www.unicef.org/people/people_48227.html

https://people.com/music/ricky-martin-heartbreak-puerto-rico-crisis-i-dont-sleep/

https://www.latintimes.com/ricky-martin-kisses-woman-fan-pays-nearly-100k-lock-lips-singer-was-it-worth-it-380136

Rob Halford

http://www.mtv.com/news/1429870/rob-halford-discusses-sexuality-publicly-for-the-first-time/

https://www.rollingstone.com/t/judas-priest/

https://www.theguardian.com/music/2010/may/20/judas-priest-rob-halford-british-steel

http://teamrock.com/feature/2016-08-02/my-life-story-rob-halford-from-metal-god-to-gay-icon

https://www.grammy.com/grammys/artists/judas-priest

http://www.blabbermouth.net/news/judas-priest-s-rob-halford-i-ve-been-screaming-my-tits-off-for-38-years-now/

https://www.washingtontimes.com/news/2016/oct/13/rob-halford-judas-priest-id-be-dead-without-sobrie/

Camille Shira Angel

https://rabbiangel.com/meet-usfs-new-rabbi-in-residence/

https://rabbiangel.com/new-lesbian-rabbi-brings-lgbtq-issues-to-forefront-at-university-of-san-francisco/

https://rabbiangel.com/about/

https://www.usfca.edu/magazine/december-2020/features/does-faith-have-a-future

https://rabbiangel.com/video-psr/

https://rabbiangel.com/meeting-the-obamas/

https://rabbiangel.com/services/

https://usfblogs.usfca.edu/strengthtolove/a-reflection-on-rev-dr-kings-sermon-transformed-nonconformist/

https://jweekly.com/2022/04/12/go-ahead-say-gay-thats-what-i-do-every-day/

https://sfbos.org/ftp/uploadedfiles/bdsupvrs/resolutions00/r0992-00.pdf

https://jweekly.com/2015/06/26/departing-shaar-zahav-rabbi-gets-oodles-of-accolades/

https://www.newwaysministry.org/2019/08/22/new-lesbian-rabbi-brings-lgbtq-issues-to-forefront-at-university-of-san-francisco/

https://jwa.org/rabbis/narrators/angel-camille

Archbishop Carl Bean

http://www.sandiegouniontribune.com/sdut-lgbt-foundation-honors-advocates-2015nov05-story.html

https://ufcmlife.org/leadership

https://www.poz.com/article/Carl-Bean-HIV-20150-6208

https://lasentinel.net/carl-bean-i-was-born-this-way.html

http://minorityaidsproject.org/founder/

Bishop V. Gene Robinson

https://www.washingtonpost.com/local/announcing-divorce-gay-bishop-gene-robinson-cites-missed-opportunities/2014/05/05/7c28849c-d485-11e3-aae8-c2d44bd79778_story.html

https://www.youtube.com/watch?v=HqvcPa-BbLc

https://www.youtube.com/watch?v=jlUs4ITbJXo

https://www.episcopalnewsservice.org/2017/05/22/gene-robinson-named-to-two-chautauqua-institution-posts/

https://www.americanprogress.org/issues/religion/news/2010/03/24/7473/get-to-know-bishop-gene-robinson/

https://www.britannica.com/biography/V-Gene-Robinson

http://web.stanford.edu/group/religiouslife/cgi-bin/wordpress/programs/god-believes-in-love/bishop-gene-robinson-biography/

https://www.nytimes.com/2003/11/03/us/openly-gay-man-is-made-a-bishop.html

http://www.pewforum.org/2017/08/08/gay-marriage-around-the-world-2013/

http://www.latimes.com/nation/la-na-boy-scouts-evolution-2017-story.html

https://www.theguardian.com/world/2003/oct/31/gayrights.religion

https://www.telegraph.co.uk/news/worldnews/northamerica/usa/10807887/First-openly-gay-Anglican-bishop-Gene-Robinson-announces-divorce.html

https://www.cbsnews.com/news/gay-bishop-being-honest-04-03-2004/

https://www.nytimes.com/2009/01/13/us/13prayer.html

https://www.salon.com/2007/10/25/film_on_gays/

https://www.metroweekly.com/2007/10/reel-affirmations-100255/

Lynn Conway

https://www.nytimes.com/2024/06/15/technology/lynn-conway-dead.html

https://time.com/130734/transgender-celebrities-actors-athletes-in-america/

https://apnews.com/article/lynn-conway-death-scientist-transgender-951e137
8c257bda707224686bebb0507

https://www.forbes.com/sites/jeremyalicandri/2020/11/18/ibm-apologizes-
for-firing-computer-pioneer/

https://www.independent.co.uk/news/world/americas/iphone-science-trans-
woman-lynn-conway-b2458269.html

https://www.invent.org/inductees/search?combine=lynn+conway

https://rse.org.uk/award/ieee-rse-james-clerk-maxwell-medal/

https://www.washingtonpost.com/obituaries/2024/06/13/lynn-conway-dead/

Rachel L. Levine

https://www.hhs.gov/about/leadership/rachel-levine.html

https://directory.alumni.psu.edu/s/1218/16/interior.
aspx?sid=1218&gid=4&pgid=5653&cid=28666&ecid=28666&crid=0&calpgi
d=4259&calcid=28662

https://ppimhs.org/newspost/dr-rachel-levine-a-groundbreaking-figure-in-
pennsylvanian-healthcare-history/

https://www.usatoday.com/in-depth/opinion/2022/03/13/rachel-levine-
honoree-usa-today-women-of-the-year/6600134001/

https://www.hhs.gov/about/news/2023/07/31/hhs-announces-formation-
office-long-covid-research-practice-launch-long-covid-clinical-trials-through-
recover-initiative.html

https://www.media.pa.gov/Pages/Health-Details.aspx?newsid=620

https://www.womenshistory.org/education-resources/
biographies/rachel-levine

Alan Turing

https://www.britannica.com/biography/Alan-Turing

https://www.biography.com/people/alan-turing-9512017

https://www.forbes.com/sites/daviddisalvo/2012/05/27/how-alan-turing-
helped-win-wwii-and-was-thanked-with-criminal-prosecution-for-being-
gay/#12061a5f5cc3

https://www.bbc.com/news/technology-18419691

http://www.guinnessworldrecords.com/world-records/highest-death-toll-from-wars/

https://www.history.com/topics/world-war-ii

https://paw.princeton.edu/article/top-25

Sally Ride, Ph.D.

https://www.nasa.gov/sites/default/files/atoms/files/ride_sally.pdf

https://www.space.com/16756-sally-ride-biography.html

https://www.space.com/40916-sally-ride-pride-inspiration-legacy.html

https://www.history.com/news/navy-christens-research-ship-named-for-sally-ride

https://www.history.com/news/sally-ride-first-astronaut-sexism

https://www.nasa.gov/audience/forstudents/k-4/stories/nasa-knows/who-was-sally-ride-k4.html

https://www.biography.com/people/sally-ride-9458284

https://airandspace.si.edu/collection-objects/award-ncaa-silver-anniversary-student-athlete-sally-ride

Megan Rapinoe

https://www.biography.com/athletes/megan-rapinoe

https://www.britannica.com/biography/Megan-Rapinoe

https://www.teamusa.com/profiles/megan-rapinoe-876533

https://olympics.com/en/athletes/megan-rapinoe

https://www.ussoccer.com/players/r/megan-rapinoe

https://www.nytimes.com/2019/07/10/sports/soccer/soccer-parade.html

https://www.commerce.senate.gov/2023/1/president-biden-signs-cantwell-capito-equal-pay-bill-into-law https://www.fifa.com/en/tournaments/womens/womensworldcup/australia-new-zealand2023/articles/which-team-won-last-womens-world-cup-france-2019

https://www.npr.org/transcripts/1102146428

https://www.npr.org/transcripts/933018609

https://time.com/6293102/megan-rapinoe-world-cup-2023-interview-retirement/

https://www.ussoccer.com/stories/2015/06/pinoes-biggest-fan

https://www.npr.org/2019/03/08/701522635/u-s-womens-soccer-team-sues-u-s-soccer-for-gender-discrimination

https://www.nytimes.com/2022/02/22/sports/soccer/us-womens-soccer-equal-pay.html

https://www.forbes.com/sites/brettknight/2023/07/21/womens-world-cup-highest-paid-alex-morgan-megan-rapinoe/

Billie Jean King

http://parentingaces.com/hbo-sports-billie-jean-king-portrait-pioneer/

https://www.amazon.com/Pressure-Privilege-Lessons-Learned-Library/dp/0981636802

https://www.youtube.com/watch?v=QUPI5HLLojg

https://www.youtube.com/watch?v=MyMtOwwtJW0

https://www.amazon.com/American-Masters-Billie-Jean-King/dp/B00JUIZTMM

https://www.biography.com/people/billie-jean-king-9364876

https://www.nytimes.com/2006/04/26/arts/television/the-legacy-of-billie-jean-king-an-athlete-who-demanded.html

https://www.espn.com/sportscentury/features/00016060.html

https://www.cnn.com/2014/02/24/sport/tennis/billie-jean-king-fast-facts/index.html

https://www.nbcnews.com/feature/nbc-out/it-was-horrible-billie-jean-king-recalls-being-publicly-outed-n804451 https://www.encyclopedia.com/people/sports-and-games/sports-biographies/billie-jean-king

https://www.history.com/topics/womens-history/billie-jean-king

https://www.britannica.com/biography/Billie-Jean-King

http://www.pbs.org/wnet/americanmasters/billie-jean-king-filmmaker-essay-on-billie-jean-king/2714/

http://www.nydailynews.com/sports/more-sports/billie-jean-king-confesses-1981-lesbian-article-1.2615020

https://www.si.com/sports-man/2010/11/30/billiejeanking-sportsman

https://www.si.com/si-sportsperson-history-female-winners-serena-williams

https://www.theguardian.com/world/2017/nov/12/billie-jean-king-tennis-equality-battle-of-the-sexes

https://www.phillymag.com/articles/2011/06/17/billie-jean-king-racquet-revolutionary/4/

https://www.usopen.org/en_US/news/articles/2018-08-21/50_moments_that_mattered_us_open_is_first_grand_slam_tournament_to_offer_equal_prize_money.html

https://obamawhitehouse.archives.gov/blog/2009/07/30/presidential-medal-freedom-recipients

Esera Tuaolo

http://eseratuaolo.me/biography/

https://www.glaad.org/blog/esera-tuaolo-explains-why-he-hopes-his-first-ever-super-bowl-inclusion-party-will-change-game-lgbtq-professional-sports

https://people.com/archive/gay-man-in-the-nfl-vol-65-no-9/

https://www.today.com/popculture/former-nfl-player-esera-tuaolo-wows-judges-voice-song-story-t116706

http://morristrophy.com/past-winners/players/esera-tuaolo/

https://abcnews.go.com/GMA/story?id=125632&page=1

https://www.nbc.com/the-voice/credits/credit/season-13/esera-tuaolo

https://www.npr.org/templates/story/story.php?storyId=5190140

https://www.nytimes.com/2002/10/27/sports/backtalk-toughest-play-for-veteran-of-nfl-trench-warfare.html

https://today.oregonstate.edu/archives/2003/may/osu-alum-tuaolo-speak-osu-about-nfl-life-gay-athlete

http://a.espncdn.com/nfl/news/2002/1024/1450380.html

https://www.outsports.com/2018/2/2/16962980/super-bowl-52-lgbt-inclusion-party-esera-tuaolo

Jason Collins

http://webtv.un.org/www.unwomen.org/en/executive-board/watch/martina-navratilova-and-jason-collins-on-sport-and-the-fight-against-homophobia-press-conference/2919746360001/

http://lapmf.org/events/golf-tournament/

http://www.lapdonline.org/november_2016/news_view/61440

https://www.prnewswire.com/news-releases/heroes-for-heroes-3rd-annual-los-angeles-police-memorial-foundation-celebrity-poker-tournament--casino-night-party-300513993.html

http://time.com/70898/jason-collins-2014-time-100/

https://www.si.com/more-sports/2013/04/29/jason-collins-gay-nba-player

https://www.si.com/more-sports/2013/04/29/jason-collins-reveals-gay-nba-story

https://www.bbc.com/news/world-us-canada-22341153

https://mashable.com/2013/04/30/jason-collins-sports-illustrated-traffic/

https://www.nytimes.com/2014/03/03/sports/basketball/jason-collins-brooklyn-debut-recalls-jackie-robinsons-in-1947.html

https://pac-12.com/article/2001/05/07/stanfords-jason-collins-declares-nba-draft

https://www.buzzfeed.com/driadonnaroland/nba-will-donate-sales-of-jason-collins-jersey-to-lgbt-groups

https://www.si.com/nba/2016/11/01/jason-collins-hillary-clinton-election-campaign-trail

https://www.healthiergeneration.org/articles/chelsea-clinton-jillian-michaels-and-leading-health-advocates-honor-the-nations-healthiest

Stephen Alexander

https://www.outsports.com/2013/11/12/5095154/transgender-coach-stephen-alexander-profile-glocester-rhode-island

https://www.youtube.com/watch?v=NMTE1o1zLFk

https://www.si.com/vault/issue/1012641/147

http://turnto10.com/archive/only-on-10-transgendered-coach-works-at-ponagnaset-high-school

https://qsaltlake.com/news/2017/03/06/stephen-alexander-little-rhodys-big-trans-man/

http://www.valleybreeze.com/2014-08-13/observer-smithfield-west/ponaganset-hall-fame-induction-dinner-sept-27#.W1HpeLHMxE4

https://fosterponaganseths.ss11.sharpschool.com/athletics/athletic_hall_of_fame

http://www.glocesterri.org/2015Minutes.pdf

https://competenetwork.com/faces-of-sports-transgender-athlete-stephen-alexander/

https://boston.edgemedianetwork.com/news/national/152684/rhode_island_home_to_1st_transgender_high_school_coach

http://www.transyouthequality.org/about-us/

https://www.huffingtonpost.com/grace-anne-stevens/my-transgender-life-where_b_7633434.html

James Baldwin

https://www.biography.com/activists/martin-luther-king-jr-james-baldwin-relationship

https://nmaahc.si.edu/explore/stories/baldwin-france#

https://www.bbc.com/news/entertainment-arts-50302788

https://nmaahc.si.edu/explore/exhibitions/chez-baldwin/faqs

https://www.nbcnews.com/feature/nbc-out/james-baldwin-s-sexuality-complicated-influential-n717706

https://www.nytimes.com/2020/12/08/books/barack-obama-promised-land-reading-writing.html

https://nmaahc.si.edu/explore/stories/lane-literature

Mary Oliver

http://www.oprah.com/entertainment/Maria-Shriver-Interviews-Poet-Mary-Oliver

https://vimeo.com/236014103

https://www.newyorker.com/magazine/2017/11/27/what-mary-olivers-critics-dont-understand

http://blindflaneur.com/2010/08/19/mary-oliver-%E2%80%98a-bride-married-to-amazement%E2%80%99/

http://www.grolierpoetrybookshop.org/HallofFamep7.html

https://www.poetryfoundation.org/poets/mary-oliver

http://maryoliver.beacon.org/

https://www.goodreads.com/book/show/178959.American_Primitive

https://artsandletters.org/academy-members/

https://www.pulitzer.org/winners/mary-oliver

https://www.britannica.com/biography/Mary-Oliver

https://www.poets.org/poetsorg/poet/mary-oliver

https://www.goodreads.com/choiceawards/best-poetry-books-2012

http://mariashriver.com/mystory/first-lady-of-california/

https://www.independent.co.uk/news/obituaries/molly-malone-cook-310749.html

http://www.nationalbook.org/people/mary-oliver/

Oscar Wilde

https://www.nytimes.com/1998/03/26/theater/arts-abroad-the-ideal-martyr-oscar-wilde-has-the-last-laugh.html

https://www.washingtonpost.com/blogs/answer-sheet/post/irish-authors-the-10-most-read/2012/03/09/gIQAheLIDS_blog.html

http://www.dramaonlinelibrary.com/playwrights/oscar-wilde-iid-12322?start=0

https://www.biography.com/people/oscar-wilde-9531078

https://www.theguardian.com/books/2003/may/07/top10s.oscar.wilde

https://www.youtube.com/watch?v=cqRwZz7n8o8

Tony Kushner

https://www.nytimes.com/2017/09/07/theater/angels-in-america-is-returning-to-broadway-with-nathan-lane.html

http://www.imdb.com/name/nm1065785/bio?ref_=nm_ov_bio_sm

https://www.nytimes.com/2018/03/07/theater/tony-kushner-angels-in-america-broadway.html

http://time.com/5165784/angels-in-america-original-reviews/

http://variety.com/2018/legit/news/original-angels-in-america-ambitious-theater-1202706599/

https://www.britannica.com/biography/Tony-Kushner

https://study.com/academy/lesson/tony-kushner-biography-plays.html

https://www.encyclopedia.com/people/literature-and-arts/theater-biographies/tony-kushner

https://www.pulitzer.org/winners/tony-kushner

https://www.boxofficemojo.com/movies/?id=lincoln.htm

https://www.arts.gov/honors/medals/tony-kushner

https://www.oscars.org/oscars/ceremonies/2013

https://www.imdb.com/event/ev0000383/2005/1

Photo Credits

pg. 22 (Marsha P. Johnson): Alamy Stock Photo / Patsy Lynch

pg. 22 (Sylvia Rivera): Wikimedia Commons, Roseleechs

pg. 25 (Kelley Robinson): Shutterstock/lev radin

pg. 28 (Bayard Rustin): Shutterstock/AP/Jacob Harris

pg. 31 (X González): Shutterstock/lev radin

pg. 34 (Nyle DiMarco): Shutterstock/DFree

pg. 37 (Cecelia Maria Zarbo Wambach, PhD): Bobbi Ausubel

pg. 41 (Beth Ford): Alamy Stock Photo / USDA Photo

pg. 44 (Rick Welts): Alamy Stock Photo / Sipa USA

pg. 47 (Suze Orman): Shutterstock/s_bukley

pg. 49 (Tim Cook): Shutterstock/Laura Hutton

pg 54 (Frida Kahlo): Wikimedia Commons, Guillermo Kahlo

pg. 58 (Bill T. Jones): Shutterstock/BEI/Carolyn Contino

pg. 61 (Jin Xing): Shutterstock/Jonathan Browning

pg. 65 (RuPaul): Shutterstock/Kathy Hutchins

pg. 68 (Hannah Gadsby): Shutterstock/Kathy Hutchins

pg. 71 (Ariana DeBose): Shutterstock/Fred Duval

pg. 74 (Daniela Vega): Shutterstock/Cineberg

pg. 77 (Robin Roberts): Shutterstock/Leonard Zhukovsky

pg. 80 (Chris Nee): Shutterstock/AP/Invision/Charles Sykes

pg. 83 (Sir Ian McKellen): Shutterstock/magicinfoto

pg. 85 (Margaret Cho): Shutterstock/s_bukley

pg. 88 (The Wachowskis): Shutterstock/Variety/David Buchan and Shutterstock/DFree

pg. 91 (Harvey Millk): Alamy Stock Photo / Robert Clay

pg. 94 (Mary Yu): Office of Governor Inslee

pg 97 (Pete Buttigieg): Shutterstock/Trevor Bexon

pg. 100 (Jóhanna Sigurðardóttir): Alamy Stock Photo / The Picture Art Collection

pg. 103 (Leo Varadkar): Shutterstock/Alexandros Michailidis

pg. 106 (Eric Fanning): Shutterstock/Epa/Shawn Thew

pg. 109 (Technical Sergeant Leonard P. Matlovich): Brandon Wolf

pg. 113 (Brandi Carlile): Shutterstock/Carl Beust

pg. 116 (Sir Elton John): Shutterstock/Featureflash Photo Agency

pg. 119 (k.d. Lang): Shutterstock/Paul McKinnon

pg. 122 (Leonard Bernstein): Shutterstock/AP/Anonymous

pg. 125 (Ricky Martin): Shutterstock/DFree

pg. 128 (Rob Halford): Shutterstock/Northfoto

pg. 132 (Camille Shira Angel): Camille Shira Angel

pg. 135 (Archbishop Carl Bean): Flickr / Emery Taylor

pg. 138 (Bishop V. Gene Robinson): Shutterstock/EPA/C.j. Gunther

pg. 142 (Lynn Conway): Wikimedia Commons / Photo by Charles Rogers

pg. 145 (Rachel L. Levine): Alamy Stock Photo / UPI

pg. 148 (Alan Turing): Alamy Stock Photo / CPA Media Pte Ltd

pg. 151 (Sally Ride, PhD): Shutterstock/mark reinstein

pg. 155 (Megan Rapinoe): Shutterstock/Jose Breton-Pics Action

pg. 158 (Billie Jean King): Shutterstock/Krista Kennell

pg. 161 (Esera Tuaolo): Shutterstock/BEI/Matt Baron

pg. 164 (Jason Collins): Shutterstock/s_bukley

pg. 167 (Stephen Alexander): Eric Rosswood

pg. 171 (James Baldwin): Album / Alamy Stock Photo

pg. 175 (Mary Oliver): Shutterstock/AP/MARK LENNIHAN

pg. 178 (Oscar Wilde): Shutterstock/Everett Historical

pg. 181 (Tony Kushner): Shutterstock/Ga Fullner

Mango Publishing, established in 2014, publishes an eclectic list of books by diverse authors—both new and established voices—on topics ranging from business, personal growth, women's empowerment, LGBTQ+ studies, health, and spirituality to history, popular culture, time management, decluttering, lifestyle, mental wellness, aging, and sustainable living. We were named 2019 *and* 2020's #1 fastest growing independent publisher by *Publishers Weekly*. Our success is driven by our main goal, which is to publish high-quality books that will entertain readers as well as make a positive difference in their lives.

Our readers are our most important resource; we value your input, suggestions, and ideas. We'd love to hear from you—after all, we are publishing books for you!

Please stay in touch with us and follow us at:

Facebook: Mango Publishing

Twitter: @MangoPublishing

Instagram: @MangoPublishing

LinkedIn: Mango Publishing

Pinterest: Mango Publishing

Newsletter: mangopublishinggroup.com/newsletter

Join us on Mango's journey to reinvent publishing, one book at a time.

Printed in the USA
CPSIA information can be obtained
at www.ICGtesting.com
JSHW030027151124
73615JS00001B/1